The Cowboy's Secret Babies

The Cowboy's Secret Babies

A Careys of Cowboy Point Novel

Megan Crane

TULE

Prologue

Z EKE CAREY ENDED the call, slipped his mobile into his pocket, and congratulated himself on yet another pitch-perfect performance.

He'd clearly missed his true calling.

But that notion made him laugh, because he was nothing if not a rancher. These wild Montana acres were as much a part of him as his own old, creaky bones. There was no part of this land he didn't love. It had been in the family for generations and he intended to see to it that it would stay in the family for generations more.

He had gone to great lengths to make sure that it would, and he didn't regret it one bit.

It wasn't every man who would tell his own sons that he was dying when he wasn't, and more, that his dying wish was to see all five of them married with some kids on the way.

Zeke prided himself on being the kind of father who always went that extra mile.

He was already two down. There were three more of his obstinate sons to go, all of them chips off the old block by his estimation, so he knew exactly how to get around the unique orneriness each one of the five brought to the table.

That was what the call had been about. Zeke had put on an Oscar-worthy performance. He'd stood out here in the barn, talking in a feeble voice like he'd taken to his bed, and interrupted himself by wafting off into the odd coughing fit.

One of these days he was going to bust a rib and rip up his own throat with these games, but even then he'd consider it all worthwhile.

Particularly in this case. His prodigal son was coming home.

It was about damn time.

Zeke finished up the few small tasks he'd come out to the barn to handle. He walked over to the barn door and set about shrugging on his cold-weather gear to brave the winter outside, because even the short walk back to the house was too much at this time of year. Last night's storm had dumped a few extra feet on the existing snowdrifts, plumping them up nice and high, but that was February. And these were the mountains.

And only a deep and abiding fool—or a tourist from somewhere warmer—underestimated a Rocky Mountain winter.

Zeke was a lot of things, but he'd never been much of a fool. Or a tourist, for that matter.

And a man who'd given his life to the land wasn't likely to risk it in a little snow. He zipped up his parka and stepped out into the cold.

These days, it was his boys who made sure that there was

a shoveled path between the old ranch house and the barn. Zeke didn't even have to ask. Every time it snowed, one of his sons was out there before it stopped, making sure that Zeke and his beloved wife Belinda didn't have to worry about a thing.

This confirmed for Zeke that he'd raised them all right. It was a funny thing, bringing up a pack of boys and hoping to make them into good men. You couldn't do anything but your best, whatever that looked like from one season to the next, and hope it worked out in the end.

So far, Zeke thought it was working out pretty damn great. He'd already managed to get two of his sons married off.

Harlan was the oldest, a stalwart and dependable man who reminded Zeke the most of Alice, Zeke's first wife. She'd been a rock, too, while she was still with them. The only surprising thing Harlan had done in his life was marry Kendall by putting out an old-fashioned ad, but they'd been together for almost a year now. A perfect match.

And if Zeke wasn't mistaken—a great rarity, he liked to think, though he knew better than to say such things in the presence of his tempestuous wife—Kendall had been looking a little pale lately. She'd had less of an appetite at Sunday dinner. When asked, she always said she was doing great.

But Zeke had seen two different women carry a Carey child and he was pretty sure he knew the signs. He'd already told Belinda his suspicions, so he could also bask in how correct he was when Harlan and Kendall finally made an announcement.

A happy ending that kept getting more happy.

His second son, the oldest of his twins, had gotten married back in the fall. Wilder had always loved living up to his name, so it had taken the forbidden youngest daughter of the Carey family's longstanding rivals to sort him out. Leave it to Wilder to not simply find a woman but to find the one woman in the state of Montana that he really shouldn't go near, thanks to *generations* of bad blood between the two families.

But every time Zeke saw Wilder and Cat together, they looked happier.

And no need to ask us if we're having babies, Cat had told them all herself at Christmas. The two formerly feuding families had come together for what should have been an awkward sort of holiday party, but wasn't, because once they all started talking about the great many things they had in common, even the Careys and the Lisles had more than enough to talk about.

Because you already are? Belinda had asked, making no attempt to hide the way she was eyeing Cat's figure.

Because it's rude, Wilder had told his stepmother, though without heat.

And also because we are definitely not even getting pregnant until we've been married at least *a year*, Cat had told the whole room, with that smile on her face that Zeke suspected meant she wanted to poke at her older brothers. *Because I know this entire town thinks we got married because Wilder knocked me up.*

Everyone except Dallas and me, her oldest brother, Tennessee, had said in his stern, unamused way. *Because if he did, he'd be dead.*

Merry Christmas to you too, brother, Wilder had said merrily, and had toasted his in-laws.

"It's all good," Zeke said out loud as he navigated the path through the snow. "It's only going to get better now."

And when the wind picked up, it sounded like a song, and he knew that was his Alice. Checking in and letting him know that she was with him, still and always. That she approved of what he'd done so far.

Not to mention what was to come.

"You'll see," he told the wind. His lost, first love. "They're going to be happy, my love. Just like we were."

It had been a dark, late morning. A gloomy day. And now it was fixing to be another long, stormy night. There was already snow coming down as he made his way back from the barn toward the house, but it never failed to make his heart sing a little bit in his chest. The beauty of this place, even covered in winter, that he knew enough to make sure he got out in as often as he could.

Because men who worked the land weren't meant to be house pets. That he knew. And in winter, folks who lived in places where winter clamped down hard and held on tight, it was necessary to get out there and enjoy the weather no matter how grim it got.

Hibernation only worked if you were a bear.

The lights in the windows of the house beamed out at him as he drew close, beckoning a man in.

He stomped his way into the mudroom, peeled off the heavy outer layers that kept the cold at a reasonable level, and padded into the kitchen in his heavy winter socks. The heat of the house made his cold cheeks feel even colder at first, though they warmed as he made his way inside.

Belinda was sitting at the kitchen table, looking through some papers. There was a big spread of the bespoke spurs and bits that were Zeke's hobby, gleaming in the light. More than just a hobby now, Zeke thought. That was thanks to Kendall and the booth she'd set up for him at the summer market, and the website she'd built for him too. Things he'd never thought he'd ever do.

Everything around here was changing. For the better.

"Ryder's coming home," he told his wife.

Belinda looked up from her stack of papers, a grin breaking across her face. "You really sold it at Christmas. Clutching that blanket around your shoulders like the next draft might take you out was a nice touch."

"It was some of my best work," Zeke agreed.

Belinda's grin widened as she gazed at him, another sure-fire way to get that song going in his heart.

Zeke was an extraordinarily lucky man. Alice had been a

gem. An angel. She had made everything around her better until the day she'd died. Now he spent a lot of time talking to her, and saw the signs she sent him in return, as they both watched over their grown sons.

He had never stopped loving her. He never would.

Belinda was more of a storm. She still swept him away with that smile of hers. She had taken on his first three boys as if they were her own, helped him raise them, and had always treated them like they were no different from the two younger boys she went on to make with him. She had never begrudged his love of Alice, or demanded he get over it.

On the contrary, Belinda grew flowers in the warmer months for Zeke to put on Alice's grave. In the colder months, she drove down into Marietta to get arrangements from the florist.

Zeke's life had almost too much love to bear.

So why not add more? Why not pack it as full as it could get?

"Do you know how hard it is for me to see those little boys in town?" Belinda was asking, her grin fading a bit as she shook her head. "I don't know how I didn't see it myself."

"I imagine because Rosie didn't want any of us to see it," Zeke said, mildly enough.

Though this was not a topic he felt *mildly* about, he knew it wouldn't do them any good to get Belinda too riled up.

Belinda truly *riled* was far more worrisome than any *storm*, as he could attest, having done his share of riling her up over time.

It had been late in the fall when he'd figured out the truth. Rosie Stark, a member of an old Cowboy Point family, had shocked the whole community a few years back by coming home after her college graduation pregnant.

With twins, no less, and Zeke had spent a good amount of time kicking himself for not cluing into that. She had a pair of identical boys, had never mentioned the father, as far as anyone could tell, and flatly refused to engage in any of the rumors surrounding her.

Zeke hadn't thought much of it—aside from the usual pleasure he took in psychoanalyzing his friends and neighbors, a particular joy in a small town where a man could be sure he was providing everyone around him with a similar narrative. Not, that was, until the day that Zeke ran into her and her boys in the store and recognized the dark eyes staring back at him from a little boy's face.

Alice's eyes.

More to the point, his three oldest sons' eyes.

Zeke had known immediately whose babies those were. For one thing, it was clear that Rosie had gotten pregnant down in Austin, where she'd been at school. There was only one of Zeke's sons who spent any time in Texas, because Ryder had gone off chasing the rodeo when he was still a teenager himself and Texas was one of the places he apparently liked better than home, he was there so much.

He had Belinda had gone round and round on that one, too.

He needs to do right by those babies and that girl, Belinda would mutter in bed at night, glaring at the ceiling while they curled into each other after making sure the sheets were nice and rumpled. *All three of us raised him better than this.*

Because that was Belinda. Always making sure Alice was a part of this family she'd helped make.

I don't think he knows, Zeke usually said after these rants of hers. All focused on the horror of thinking one of her boys was a deadbeat, in the end. The shame of it would kill her, she was sure—but she planned to make sure Ryder felt it too.

He will, Belinda would say, darkly. *Believe you me, he will know.*

Zeke couldn't believe that Ryder *could* know. Ryder was a big rodeo star these days and Zeke had a good idea what sort of attention went along with that, especially from women, but this was still Ryder they were talking about. The child who'd always had a strict code that he'd adhered to from birth, more or less.

He wouldn't tattle. What he would do was claim that any wrongdoing was his if he thought he could take fire from one of his brothers. Always happy to take the fall, even when innocent, that was Ryder.

Because, like every other member of the Carey family, Ryder secretly believed he alone was the tough one. Zeke was familiar with the pathology, having had it pointed out to him sweetly—but consistently—by one wife, and a whole lot louder by another.

No way would Ryder let Rosie suffer. That was the thing. Relationships were complicated, but Ryder would never let a woman with *his* babies worry where her kids' next meal was coming from. He would never leave anyone exposed to town gossip and scandal thanks to him. That wasn't how he was made.

It had been tempting to tell him straight out.

But Zeke had decided they needed a plan. They couldn't demand that Ryder come home without telling him why. And Zeke and Belinda agreed—eventually—that Rosie and Ryder had to be the ones to have the conversation. It wouldn't help any to insert themselves.

He'll either know those little boys are his on sight or he's an idiot, Belinda had said. *As I plan to tell him myself.*

Besides, there was Rosie herself to consider.

Cowboy Point was a small place. Zeke had known Rosie her whole life, and her parents for their whole lives too. Belinda was friendly with Rosie's mother, the dreamy, impractical Charlotte who was forever declaring that she had *entered a new era* and therefore had a new name to go with it.

Most recently, if Zeke was keeping up, *Moonshadow.*

Moonshadow Stark, of all things.

How a flighty woman like Charlotte had ever married Jimmy Stark, who had been curmudgeonly even when he

10

was small, no one would ever know. He had shuffled off the mortal coil far too young and left no answers behind him. Just three kids spread out over some fifteen years. Rosie was the youngest.

Charlotte Moonshadow, or whatever she was calling herself these days, spent most of her time out in the hippie enclaves deeper into the mountains with like-minded folks. Art, she liked to say, usually without solicitation, was what called her to rise each morning and face the new day. And art was what lulled her to sleep again at night.

Zeke had no squabble with art. He'd always made his own. It had never been clear to him what Charlotte's art *was*.

She could usually be found talking intently about intentional communities, festivals of authenticity—whatever those were—and communal experiences whenever a person happened to stray too close to her in a public place. Zeke kept his distance.

Belinda liked to get as close as possible, mostly so she could report back on the state of New Age Nonsense Ranch, which was not, sadly, the actual name of the spread an hour deeper into the hills and over unmarked dirt roads from Cowboy Point. It was called Nepenthe Creek, though Zeke liked to pretend he couldn't remember that.

Charlotte was about as untethered to reality as a person could be without requiring medical intervention. Rosie, on the other hand, had always been practical and levelheaded. It hadn't surprised anyone that when she left for school after high school, she was one of the few who didn't come crawling back within the year. She was the sort of kid that everyone expected would stay gone. Visiting at the holidays, but building a life somewhere far away from this tiny little mountain community.

Rosie Stark coming back home as a single mom had never been on anyone's bingo card.

Belinda moved toward him there in the kitchen and Zeke wrapped her up in his arms, automatically. Then, when she was close, he tucked her against him and felt the way their bodies immediately melted into one.

There was no end to it, this dance of theirs.

How could he not want this for his own sons? Especially with a girl like Rosie, who had always had that core of steel in her. She'd need it, with a man as skittish as Ryder had always been.

Zeke wasn't above teaching Ryder a few of the necessary steps, just to help him along. The only trick would be doing it without Ryder catching on to the fact that Zeke knew about those babies before he did, and kept it close.

But as Zeke held Belinda close, swaying back and forth in their cozy, brightly lit kitchen to the music only the two of them could hear—while the snow came tumbling down outside and somewhere down south, rodeo hero Ryder Carey was finally headed back home to stay a while and meet his future head-on—he liked his chances.

Chapter One

RYDER CAREY TOOK the turn off of the snowy interstate too fast, then had to slow way down as he transitioned onto the smaller county road. It was that or welcome himself home in a ditch, face-first in a snowdrift, for all the locals to discuss instead of, say, his rodeo career.

Not really what he was going for.

If he had to come back to Cowboy Point, he figured he might as well ride what so-called stardom he had. In his experience, that might get a man a beer. Once.

It wasn't like a bull rider was all that exciting outside the ring. Devoid of context, he was just another guy in cowboy boots and a Stetson. A bull rider wasn't a hero, like a firefighter.

The only life Ryder had ever tried to save was his own.

Thoughts like that, he knew, were only going to lead to an immediate sit down with his ghosts, and he was already moving home for a spell. No need to rush into meetups with the inevitable specters from his childhood.

It was a bright blue February day, as pretty as it was cold. Once he was certain his Airstream wouldn't slither right off the snow-packed road, he pulled the shearling collar of his favorite coat up higher on his neck. Then shook his head at the fact he was cold at all. That was what he got for leaving Montana pretty much the moment he turned eighteen, and for wisely spending the bulk of his winters in places that smelled like flowers all year long.

Thin blood and a lot of texts from his twin brother, all designed to make him feel like an asshole for not moving on home to live on the ranch and be *one of those Carey brothers* for all eternity.

It wasn't that he didn't like his brothers. He loved them. All of them.

Still, he'd wanted to see more of the world than what was available on the backside of a mountain in Paradise Valley, MT, miles away from everything. No matter how pretty it was.

He wasn't all that happy about returning now, but he was doing it.

Finally, Wilder had texted him when Ryder had told him that yes, he was finally coming home and *yes*, he intended to stay. A while.

There was no end date because no one knew how long it would take.

It was a part of life, Ryder knew that. People got old and died. He'd watched this cycle play out in the rodeo more times than he'd like. He'd always fancied himself pretty practical where these things were concerned.

But it was different when the dying man in question was

the father he'd idolized his entire life. The one he'd always believed was immortal, because how could Zeke be anything else? Everything about him was larger than life could ever dream of becoming.

He hadn't stayed away because he didn't care. It was the opposite.

"Now you're back," he told himself, like saying the words out loud would make it better. He reminded himself of the vow he'd made when he'd left what might have been his last rodeo in Texas a few days earlier—though he wasn't sure he was ready to pull that trigger, not yet, no matter how much his damn body hurt these days. He'd told himself that *this time*, in honor of his father, he would leave the historic chip on his shoulder behind for once.

But there it was, sure enough, pressing down on his trapezoid muscles like an anvil.

Like it planned to stay a while.

He drove along the outskirts of the small town of Marietta, nestled there in the inarguably beautiful Paradise Valley about an hour or so south of Livingston. As a teenager, he'd raced along these roads as fast as he could go, like he was trying to outrun the Gallatins themselves. Those were the mountains that started down in Yellowstone and stretched all the way up to Livingston, forming the western wall of the valley.

Somehow, he always forgot the way it was when he was near them. How they seemed to sing their way inside him.

That chip on his shoulder only got heavier as he aimed his truck and trailer up the side of Copper Mountain, all covered in snow, which made it a certainty that the winding, ten-mile stretch of road that meandered its way to the back side of the mountain would be slick and dangerous.

"Good times," he muttered.

Not that it was the weather that was really bothering him. He didn't even mind it when the wind picked up halfway into the slow climb, kicking around the already-fallen snow like it wanted to welcome him home with a trusty ground blizzard. Just to say hello, Montana-style.

The trouble was that he was coming home at all.

Ryder had spent the better part of his adult life avoiding ever visiting for more than a quick weekend, and even that as seldom as possible. It wasn't that he hated this place, he admitted to himself as he crested the last rise and got a good look at the even smaller valley that waited there on the other side. Truth was, he didn't. He couldn't.

But he preferred to keep his distance all the same.

This afternoon, with the sky so blue and the tiny community of Cowboy Point spread out below him like a painting, it was hard to remember why.

Ryder drove down the far gentler slope on the far side of the mountain, through waiting lines of evergreens with snow weighing their branches down. The road wasn't plowed—there was no point in it, not this high up—but the snow beneath his tires was packed tight and didn't feel icy or treacherous.

Snow made everything feel closer, cozier. The last time he'd been home had been a whirlwind trip to make it to Wilder's shotgun wedding. It had been an achingly crisp and beautiful fall, gold and orange and red. It had hurt a little, if he was honest. So had seeing his twin so happy, for all the right reasons.

Today, there were feet of snow piled high, everywhere he looked.

He could see the lights on in the library and in the elementary school, working hard to ward off the bitter cold and the dark that fell hard and quick. Farther down the road, the cluster of buildings that made up what passed for a town boasted even more lights. In the little shops, strung along the roofs, anything to beat back the northern winter dark. Because this time of year, spring always seemed too far away.

Higher in the hills that rose above the narrow valley that made up Cowboy Point, he could see more points of light in the houses that clung to the hillsides and up high on Lisle Hill, where some maniac Lisle had built himself a lighthouse. Some eight hundred miles from the sea.

A lighthouse that was no longer the beacon of his family's enemies, he reminded himself. Given the fact that Wilder had gone ahead and married one of them.

He crossed over the frozen creek, considered a spot of day drinking at the always-open Copper Mine, but kept driving. No point in making things worse by dragging it all out.

On the far side of the small valley, the road led him up another hill and he blew out a breath as he passed the lodge that had stood tall at the top for more than a hundred years. It had been closed for most of Ryder's life, victim to disputes within the family that owned it. It was still closed, as far as he knew, though he could see lights on inside its graceful old windows too, and had a vague memory of someone at Wilder's wedding telling him that Jack Stark, the oldest Stark cousin in Ryder's generation, had big plans to revamp the place and get it up and running again.

From what he could remember about Jack, he always had big plans, and yet here he still was in this tiny speck of a place that only made some maps, and only the ones that zoomed in.

For the sake of the community, Ryder hoped that the extended Stark family who communally owned it—or so the rumors went—had finally gotten their act together the way their parents had not. Thinking about the Stark family did not make him feel better about this whole homecoming situation, however.

Well. It was only the one member of the Stark family that made his chest feel a little too tight—but this wasn't the time to think about Rosie. Or that night in Austin that he really shouldn't think about as much as he did.

Ryder hated regret and avoided apologies, but he'd long since accepted the fact that if he was ever home for long enough—and if Rosie Stark was still around, which would surprise him, because pretty as it was, Cowboy Point was nothing but a wide space in a little-traveled road—he owed her one.

A man should know better than to treat a girl next door like a buckle bunny. No matter how she'd responded when he'd pulled her into his arms.

That was on him. And he'd say so, if he ever saw her again.

He had to believe he was still that much of a man, despite what his brothers liked to tell him.

Thinking about Rosie was a good way to *not* think about where he was headed, a problem he had encountered more than once over the years since that night, but soon enough he was there anyway.

High Mountain Ranch. Home.

Ryder squared his shoulders and guided his truck onto the acreage that had been in his family since crusty old Matthew Carey made it all the way to Montana, failed at being a miner, grew an epic mustache, and decided to try his hand at cattle instead.

"You're being ridiculous," he muttered at himself.

That was true. He knew it was true.

But he still didn't want to be here.

Something he had tried to make clear to his brothers, who were famous for not listening to him.

Especially his twin.

You need to come home, Wilder had said at Christmas.

Not in a text that time, but to his face. *It's time.*

It can't be time, Ryder had replied in his usual glib fashion. Or anyway, he'd smiled blandly at his brother, and had acted as if he had no idea that Wilder's tone had gotten… intense. *I have bulls to ride, bunnies to buckle. It's hard being the pretty one.*

Because that was what he always said.

Because it was always true.

What you have, his twin had replied in a low voice that Ryder didn't like at all, because it was serious and they made a point of never being too serious, *is one sick father. You're going to regret it if all you remember of his last year is not being here.*

But Wilder was the dramatic twin. Ryder probably would have blown what he'd said off if he hadn't talked to Harlan.

Harlan was the most dependable. That was why he was in charge. It was true that his brother Boone was a close second in the dependability department, and the next in line age-wise after Ryder, but Harlan was the one that Ryder trusted the most.

Harlan was the one everyone trusted the most, because Harlan was the one who always told the truth. Like it or not.

Unlike Wilder, Harlan also didn't exaggerate.

Do you think I need to come home? he'd asked Harlan while they were out chopping wood on Christmas night.

His older brother had held his gaze a little bit too long,

the snow coming down hard and the light from inside not quite doing its job.

I do, he'd said quietly. *And soon.*

That had really cinched it. Ryder hadn't stayed home then and there. He couldn't. He'd made commitments to the tour and that meant there were still bulls to ride, as he'd said.

But now it was February. It was a good stopping place, if a man wanted to stop—or needed to press the pause button. A lot of bull riders took off part of the winter anyway, depending on what tour they were signed with. The American Extreme Bull Riders Tour that Ryder had headlined for years now took a break this time of year, then came back in the spring.

Ryder figured he could do the same this year instead of heading down south toward good weather and a beach the way he usually did.

Assuming, that was, that their father was actually as bad as Wilder claimed.

The trouble was, Ryder had the sinking feeling that he was. It was bad enough that Zeke had acted so frail over Christmas, sitting in a chair with a blanket pulled over him like he was feeling the draft from death's door and was holding it off with a flannel shroud.

Maybe the reality he really didn't want to face was that it was happening. It was happening, it was bad, and there was no bargaining that away.

When he thought about Zeke's condition, it made sense that he was here. When he thought about the fact that his father might actually be dying the way he'd told them all he was last Easter, well.

Ryder knew he was doing the right thing.

He just wished he didn't have to do it.

As he drove along the dirt road that wound its lazy way into the heart of the ranch and up to the sprawling old house where he'd grown up, he didn't follow it all the way up. There were little dirt roads that pulled off here and there, and he could see smoke coming from the various chimneys that marked the individual cabins that were tucked away in the trees and the rolling hills.

This was where most of his brothers lived, out of sight of each other because a grown man liked a little privacy even here on the family land. But they also liked to stay close enough so that they could all easily pitch in on the ranch work the way Careys had for generations.

Ryder had nothing against ranch work. It was hard, physical labor and the truth was, he'd always liked it. He'd just always also wanted *more*. Maybe it was because he was the middle son. He'd known from a very young age that if he ever wanted anything attached to his name that was only his, he had to leave this place to get it.

Today, he passed the turnoff to the piece of land that he'd chosen when he and Wilder had turned eighteen, but had yet to build on. He kept going, and turned down

Wilder's little road instead.

And then there was no getting around it. He was here. He was home.

The moment Wilder saw his truck out front of his cabin, there would be no pretending otherwise. No backing out.

Ryder parked. Then he pushed his way out of the truck and stretched, letting the frigid air slice straight through him with all its teeth. He pulled his cowboy hat down on his head and thought it was a little too familiar, the way his boots crunched into the snow. It was the same as the kick of frigid air against his skin, like a burn.

He was barely halfway across the yard when the front door opened and there was Wilder himself, standing there with the light from inside spilling out all around him, but grinning ear to ear and much brighter.

Idiot, Ryder thought, but he felt the same swell of *rightness* he always did when he and Wilder were sharing space. They didn't have to talk about it. It was just…the way things always had been. Twin stuff.

"You made it," Wilder said, but he was shaking his head. "I expected you to call me from somewhere warm and say you'd changed your mind. That you needed a little R and R down in the Keys or some shit."

"I did change my mind. But I came anyway." Ryder eyed his twin. "I hope you're happy."

Wilder laughed, because he was one of the few people alive who didn't find Ryder formidable and intimidating—

the others being the rest of their immediate family, possibly another reason he didn't spend much time here—and met Ryder at the bottom of his porch stairs.

"I am happy. It's about time." He clapped Ryder on the back, pulled him in for a hug Ryder returned. Ungraciously. Then Wilder laughed louder at the expression on his twin's face. "I know, I know. Just look at this winter wonderland all around you. What a nightmare."

"You've been here too long. It's too cold. Humans aren't meant to live under five feet of snow for months on end."

Wilder smirked. "And you, famous rodeo star Ryder Carey, are forced to stay here against your will. What a tragedy. How will you ever survive?"

Ryder shoulder checked his twin as he richly deserved, then smiled past him to where his sister-in-law had come out to stand in the doorway to their little cabin.

"Cat," he said, and tipped his hat in her direction, opting not to pay close attention to how red-cheeked she was, suggesting that they'd been having a happy little afternoon before he showed up. That he'd interrupted them pleased him. Why should Wilder have any fun? Ryder knew he wouldn't. Not around here. "A pleasure to see you. And if I didn't say this at the wedding, it's a great pity you married so beneath yourself."

"I tell her every day that she could do better," Wilder said happily, coming up to the door and grinning at his wife. "She's ornery, though. Keeps claiming she'll stay if she wants to stay, thank you very much."

"I'm a Lisle," Cat replied, her eyes gleaming. "In the tradition of my people, I don't pay that much attention to the opinions of Careys."

"Oh, this isn't an opinion," Ryder said, and made himself laugh the way Wilder did. Like maybe this time it might take. "It's a fact. You're doomed."

"Oh no," Cat said, grinning up at her husband. "Whatever will I do?"

"Good news," Wilder said, turning back to Ryder as he pulled Cat into his side. "You're doomed with us now. Like it or not."

"I don't like it at all," Ryder declared, but more to the mountains than his brother, because Wilder wasn't paying attention.

But the Gallatins kept their own counsel, and he was back in Montana for the foreseeable future, so Ryder sucked it up and followed them both inside.

Chapter Two

ROSIE STARK'S LUCK ran out on a frigid cold February afternoon in the middle of another snowstorm.

Before that, it was a perfectly nice day in the frozen north in the middle of another winter that would never end, and that she would forget all about once it was June and light all the time.

The twins, finally recovered from the sniffles that had plagued them for most of January, slept well the night before. They hadn't gotten her up all night long, a miracle, and had managed to go without any meltdowns all morning. Levi, the bossier of the two, was ordering the younger Eli around in that toddler babble that only the two of them understood. Though more and more these days, there were English words sprinkled in there as well, Rosie always wondered if they'd also keep their secret language.

She hoped so.

She had just put them down for their afternoon nap, the most glorious part of her day. Today there had been only minimal whining and false claims of alertness.

Levi needed to be told he could not get out of bed until he counted to a hundred, which he couldn't.

Eli needed a song.

Once they were asleep, Rosie stayed there for a moment, amazed that her heart could ache so much at the sight of those little round cheeks of theirs while simultaneously despairing at how grown-up they already looked to her now that they weren't tiny babies.

Not that she could remember much about them as tiny babies, because that part of her life had been such a blur. She still didn't know how she made it through, only that she had.

And always will, she reminded herself stoutly, because she had to. And there was something marvelously freeing about not having any choice in the matter.

Rosie *would* make it through, no matter what.

She was a mother now.

After a little more admiring their ridiculous dark eyelashes and their perfect little mouths—particularly cute when they were quiet, it had to be said—she left them sleeping in her bed. They thought it was fancy and special somehow, and this got them more excited to nap, so she was all about it.

Rosie spent the next ten minutes or so moving through the house quickly, neatening up the inevitable toy explosions, throwing in some laundry, and putting the living room back to rights. It wasn't only that she liked to clean house, though she did. It was that she didn't live by herself with the boys.

And she knew perfectly well that if she let things get out

of hand, her sister Matilda would take that as an opportunity to never pick up a thing again. And likely to start moving in some of the many animals she liked to rescue, so it would truly be a zoo.

Rosie had been forced to let go of a lot of things over the past few years. She'd had to get comfortable with releasing expectation, accepting *what was* instead *what ought to have been*. It had sucked. She'd done any number of the irritating exercises she found online, all in an effort to convince herself that she was exactly where she was meant to be and all was well.

All *was* well, but she knew now that things could change. Fast.

Overnight, even.

But she did have some standards, despite the things a few gross men and even more judgmental women had said to her about her 'circumstances.' She drew the line at an actual petting zoo in the house where she lived.

When she was done restoring order, she made herself lunch. She'd whipped up a huge batch of beef stew earlier in the week when everyone knew the storm was rolling in, and she and Matilda had been eating well ever since. They could both cook, something both they and their older brother had learned pretty fast when they were kids, because it was that or not eat.

Their mother was a bighearted, deeply authentic, robustly empathetic human who actively sought and followed her own path through life.

What Charlotte was not, and never had been, was any kind of a good mother.

Rosie refused to indulge her mother's naming fetish. Charlotte called herself whatever she wanted, but that didn't mean Rosie had to go along with it. Matilda thought Rosie was being harsh, but then, Matilda and their older brother Jack had not been victimized by Charlotte when it came to their own names. Jack and Matilda were perfectly reasonable names. Teal Rose, the name that was on Rosie's birth certificate, was not.

Rosie felt perfectly justified in ignoring her mother's name changes as it suited her.

But thinking about her mother was not a good way to cultivate the peace she wanted in her life, so Rosie took her bowl of stew and a generous hunk of the bread that Matilda had baked to go along with it out into the living room, where she picked up the current book she was reading and sank into it.

With a big, happy sigh.

Sometimes she thought that really, this was the happiest she'd ever been. In these quiet moments, she loved her boys so much that she sometimes thought it would make her explode. In times like this she could sit here, not worry about bills or the price of keeping two rowdy little boys in clothes, or what latest foolishness Charlotte was certainly getting herself into right now.

There was none of the stress of college classes or those aspirations that had gone up in smoke when she'd stared down at two lines on a pregnancy test in a humid Target bathroom in Austin.

On these cozy naptime afternoons, when the boys might sleep for a solid few hours, she could simply sink into a romance novel, fill her belly, and for a little while, believe that everything was perfect.

So naturally, Matilda came stamping inside then, throwing off her coat here, her scarf there, and the one glove she appeared to still have with her on the side tale. Yet the fact that she was still wearing her brightly colored, striped knit hat seemed to escape her notice.

"Guess who's back in town," Matilda said, in that tone everyone used when they had *news*. "And it's not even a holiday."

"Some colleges have early spring breaks," Rosie said, without looking up from her book.

Because she'd already looked up and seen all of Matilda's discarded items of outerwear and knew that in a moment she would be picking it all up.

Matilda threw herself down on the couch, looking as happily disheveled as always. They looked remarkably alike as sisters, though no one ever commented on that, because they presented themselves so differently.

My night and my day, Charlotte had used to say, usually while imbibing in whatever substance was making her giddy that season.

Matilda was five years older than Rosie and was seemingly the most like Charlotte. Always floating around, leaving a trail of dishevelment in her wake, so that everyone thought she was on another planet.

The real truth was, Charlotte was something of an airhead. Matilda was not. People often confused her for one, however, because her singular focus was on animals. More to the point, she'd never bothered to figure out how to act around people.

It wasn't that she couldn't. It was that she'd never understood why she *should*.

The best thing about Matilda, Rosie had always thought, was that folks around Cowboy Point were under the impression that she was a little bit *special*. A little bit otherworldly. They thought she didn't know any better than to act the way she did, abruptly walking away from anyone who happened to be talking to her because she was bored, or because she thought she heard a kitten crying, and so on. *What can you expect from Matilda*, they would say as she drove off in her antique red truck and never seemed to suffer even a moment of social shame.

The truth was that Matilda was not neurospicy so much as she was stubborn as a mule, did exactly what she pleased at all times, and was completely immune to peer pressure or the faintest urge toward people pleasing. She just did it with an airy smile.

Rosie found it impossible not to admire her sister.

But she wasn't her.

Rosie was the baby of the family. Jack was a whole ten years older than her. After their father had died, when Rosie was only slightly older than her boys were now, he had been more of a father figure to her than a brother. He still was.

Telling *him* that she was coming home for the summer and staying there, and oh, by the way, he was going to be an uncle…

Jack hadn't been angry with her. He'd been *disappointed*.

The memory of that conversation still made her feel a little bit sweaty.

She and Matilda, on the other hand, had always been close. Rosie thought that was likely because Matilda had simply treated her like an animal in need of constant aid and attention. After all, Rosie had been nothing but a small and helpless mammal when Charlotte had brought her home. Matilda was not built to resist such creatures.

But where Matilda was perfectly happy to wander around in mismatching socks and random hand-me-downs from Jack, because she gave absolutely no thought whatsoever to her appearance, Rosie had gone in the other direction.

Before the boys, she'd been all about perfect makeup, no matter what. She'd gone to school down in Texas and had found her people there. Hair always done *just so*. No such thing as casual, not really. She considered mascara and a little bit of eyeliner as necessary to waking up as brushing her teeth or putting on clothes.

Even now, on a day where she expected to see no one and do nothing, she dressed. Rosie didn't do sweats. She liked clothes that fit her, and fit her well. She didn't do *bedraggled*. Jack took after their darker haired father while she and Matilda had the same blonde hair they'd gotten directly from Charlotte.

Ripe strawberry blonde, Charlotte liked to call it, when it was really more golden. All Rosie knew was that Matilda always had hers in two wild braids, half of it falling out all the time. Charlotte had decided on white lady dreadlocks the last time she'd come by, in a cloud of patchouli. Rosie, obviously, preferred her hair swept back into a high ponytail that looked perky, was held in perfect place with the appropriate products, and would not have looked out of place in her sorority.

"Ryder Carey," Matilda said. Seemingly out of nowhere, while Rosie had wandered off into a tangent in her head.

That name, of all names, slammed into Rosie like a bullet. But she didn't react. Not outwardly. She'd taught herself better than that, these past few years.

As always, even the thought of him set every nerve ending in her body alight. Pure hatred, she assured herself. As he richly deserved.

Her throat felt dry, so she cleared it, and wished that she could get rid of the ringing in her ears at the same time.

"What?" she managed to ask.

Matilda was frowning down at her socks, unmatched as always. She reached out and poked at one of the holes in the bright pink fabric on her left foot. "Ryder Carey came home. I was just in the general store and Tennessee Lisle said he saw Ryder pulling into town yesterday, with his trailer and all. Like he's planning to stay a while."

"Unlikely." Rosie managed to keep her voice calm, if maybe not as disinterested as she might have liked. Luckily, Matilda didn't pay attention to things like that. "He's not a hometown kind of a guy."

"He never was," Matilda agreed. "But bull riding is a mean sport. There's only so long a body can take it."

The last thing Rosie wanted to think about was Ryder Carey's *body*.

Sometimes, in the middle of the night, she liked to sit around imagining that a bull threw him, for once, and hard. That Ryder was trampled into pieces. Not enough to permanently disable him, but enough to mess up that ridiculously pretty face of his. And maybe make it impossible for him to maintain that whipcord leanness, all tight muscles, rock-hard thighs, and that ridged wonder of an abdomen that she had—

This was the wrong road to go down.

She stopped herself cold.

Rosie needed to divert this conversation away from Ryder, who could not possibly be moving back here. She couldn't accept that. It couldn't possibly be true.

She eyed her sister. "I would have thought that you'd hate bull riding. Isn't it cruel to the bulls?"

Matilda looked at Rosie like she was nuts. "Do you know how much care and maintenance goes into those bulls? First of all, they're big moneymakers. No one treats a moneymaker badly in this economy. The bulls are in perfect health. They're athletes. They're treated better than most humans, and certainly much better than any of the bull riders. If people treated stray cats the way they treated bulls at bull riding events, there wouldn't be any stray cats."

"I had no idea you were such an expert on bull riding," Rosie said, a little faintly.

"It's like we've never met. I love the rodeo." Her expression went a little dreamy, which, in Rosie's experience, led to rabbit families in the laundry room and kittens running kamikaze missions in the living room. "Maybe if Ryder really is back in town, he can bring some of that star power to the Copper Mountain Rodeo next September. I know Marietta gets superstars on the regular, but a hometown boy who hit the heights Ryder has? Think of the fundraising opportunities."

Her whole face lit up. "Maybe we could even open that shelter up here in Cowboy Point."

Rosie felt a panic attack coming on, shaped like a six-foot and something cowboy, and had to breathe deep to push it away. "Don't get ahead of yourself. You don't even know if he's friendly. Wilder is supposed to be the friendly twin. For all you know, Ryder might not even like animals."

Matilda sniffed dismissively. "Even people who don't like animals don't dare admit they don't like that in front of me. They're afraid I might get *earnest*."

This was a true thing Rosie had seen play out more than once, though she didn't find it funny just now.

Matilda chattered on about her dreams of opening up a legitimate shelter, maybe a whole veterinary office, right here in their little community. Much better than depending on the facilities that already existed down the hill in Marietta.

Ten miles down a hill that wasn't always safe to drive on.

Long after she had gone off into the kitchen to find her own bowl of stew, Rosie found herself... frozen. Her pulse was going wild in her neck, but she was unable to do much of anything except stare straight ahead like a zombie.

Ryder couldn't be home. That was impossible.

Yet even as she thought that, she knew that the real truth was that she'd been waiting on this same stretch of thin ice ever since she'd run into old Zeke Carey in the feed store that day.

The very thing she had been wanting most to avoid had happened. And so quickly that there was nothing she could have possibly done to prevent it. It was like being trapped in one of her nightmares.

Levi had gone straight to Zeke like he knew his own grandfather at a glance.

Zeke had certainly known his grandson.

Rosie had felt terrible. She still felt terrible.

She had wanted to tell him then and there, but she couldn't. How could she tell Zeke when she'd never told Ryder?

That seemed like adding insult to injury.

Rosie had spent a lot of time since then thinking a whole lot about the choices she'd made since that pivotal moment in that Target bathroom stall.

She found herself defending those choices in her head. Or in the bathroom mirror.

And every time she did, it sounded weaker.

She'd expected that Ryder would seek her out the next time he came home, if only to be polite. After all, what happened in Austin had been so…

But she didn't want to think about that night. It had caused her enough trouble already, not that she would change it now that she had Levi and Eli.

Back then, she'd thought that *at the very least*, this being such a small community, a famous man like Ryder would want to make sure that they were good. Good enough to ignore each other when they saw each other in public, that was. Good enough to make sure there would be no scenes.

But he didn't come home. And when he did, he only saw his family briefly, then left again.

Rosie intended to tell him, she really did, but he never gave her the opportunity.

And yes, sure, she knew his family. She knew exactly

where they lived. She could have tracked him down. But it all seemed so sordid and unfair when *he* never bothered to follow up after that night.

What was she supposed to do? Drop in on the Carey family while they were having Sunday dinner, announce that Ryder had knocked her up after one long night after finals week her senior year? And ask if they could maybe give her his phone number?

The very idea of it had made her want to die of shame.

And then she really did feel as if she was dying of shame, and maybe was, because she kept getting more and more pregnant.

The thing about twins was that carrying them wasn't *subtle*.

The pregnancy had been rough. They'd come early, the way twins did, and she'd spent the last month of it on bed rest. That had been a great opportunity to mourn the life she'd lost that night as well as to worry over the new life she was about to start, with two tiny babies to keep alive.

Though at least it had been a lovely change of pace from wandering around town, the subject of all the gossip.

Then, if she was brutally honest, brand-new motherhood had about killed her. And she'd had a whole lot of help. She had no idea how single mothers with no one did it, except, of course, she understood now that mothers… just figured it out.

Because they had to.

Rosie was lucky. The Starks were a big, sprawling family. Her grandparents had produced three sons. Wes, the oldest, had died only a few years ago. Jimmy, Rosie's father, had died long ago. The other uncle, Steven, was still alive, but hadn't gotten along with either of his brothers, maybe ever. He and Wes had liked to come by separately and bring up their grievances, then lay them all at Jack's feet as if he was the reincarnation of his own father.

At least all the cousins got along. Uncle Steven's three sons were feral, since their mother had run off when they were little and Steven was… not exactly nurturing. Sarah Jane, everyone's favorite cousin, was the only child of Uncle Wes. She was also Cowboy Point's librarian, a fierce advocate for every lost lamb she encountered, and she'd been a stalwart support for Rosie from the start.

The cousins had long been united in their desire to finally rehabilitate the old Cowboy Point Lodge. It was their fathers who hadn't gotten along and could never agree on a thing, so the place had fallen apart once Grandma and Grandpa Stark got too old to run it.

Jack was personally determined to give the place a new life and what Jack said usually happened.

But the second, major Stark cousin bonding experience was the twins.

Once all of her male relatives understood that Rosie wouldn't be sharing the name of the baby's father no matter how they shouted about it, they all jumped on board. The same way they did everything else.

Jack acted like the babies's father, just as he had when Rosie was a baby. Sarah Jane had moved in for the first month or two. Matilda was always good with small mammals.

Wyatt, Logan, and Noah made a game out of coming by. Rosie didn't trust her cousins not to hurt themselves, as wild as they were, but she did trust them not to hurt her boys. First they'd competed as to who was the better mother's helper in those terrifying early days. Then, as time went on, they'd taken the twins to do *man things*. Possibly *at* each other.

They would always come back with the best pictures of the twins having adventures, from fishing or hiking up some of the trails around town to pretending to help out with the lodge renovations. It was cute.

But ever since she'd run into Zeke and she'd watched him figured it out in a glance, she'd known, deep down, that she was on borrowed time.

The truth was, she always had been. She'd been kidding herself.

She could already tell that the twins looked like their daddy. Zeke wouldn't be the only one to make that connection, especially not now that Ryder was back in town. Rosie had never been anywhere near Wilder Carey and besides, even if he hadn't gone ahead and married Cat Lisle, Wilder had never been one to mess around close to home. Everyone knew his reputation, but it was made down in the Wolf Den, the seedy Marietta bar where reputations were made and drenched in whiskey, usually in the company of strangers.

Now that Ryder was back, *if* Ryder was back, people might look a little closer at Rosie's little boys.

And all of the excuses she'd used all this time were true. But it didn't matter, did it? He could have checked in with her, that was true. He'd been there that night. He knew what had happened between them.

Still, she was the one who knew that she was pregnant and she should have told him. She should have found a way. She'd let herself get wrapped up in the pregnancy. In trying to keep two perfect, active babies alive. In trying to raise them and love on them, and all the rest of it.

But a reckoning had always been coming.

Sooner or later.

Rosie couldn't breathe for the next few days. It was like she expected him to come leaping out from any shadow, and she braced herself, thinking that it would be imminent. Surely his father would have told him, if not back when he'd seen Rosie, then certainly now that he'd moved home.

By the second week after Matilda's announcement, Rosie knew that he really had moved home. Everyone knew. It was all that folks could talk about as the winter kept dragging on.

Rosie had to hear about it every time she took the twins to their cute little nursery school in the basement of the church out past the creek. She had to hear about it when she went into the general store, and every single person who came in felt called to muse on the topic with whatever member of the Lisle family was manning the till.

If she was the forthright, stand-up woman she'd always believed she was, she would handle the situation herself. She would get in her car, drive up onto the Carey's ranch, and inform Ryder of the fact that he was a father.

But try though she might, she couldn't quite bring herself to do it.

Mostly, she thought as she lay awake in her bed at night, the boys making their usual sleep noises on the baby monitor from their room across the hall, it was because she didn't want to face him.

Because the last time she'd seen him had been that morning after.

Even if she hadn't gotten pregnant that night, that particular morning would still be haunting her. That was how awful it had been. That was how intent he'd been on *making sure* that she knew she meant absolutely nothing to him, no matter what had happened between them that night.

Ryder had scraped her off like she was nothing but dirt on his cowboy boots, and she wished it was only her pride had been hurt by that. But it wasn't.

It wasn't *just* her pride, and that was the part she couldn't forget.

That was the thing that made it impossible for her to go and face him the way she should. Because she'd been foolish enough to spend that night thinking that it all *meant something*, and that was horrifying. She thought that if she had to see that pitying smile of his ever again—

But February kept moving along, and she couldn't keep herself on high alert the whole time. She had a whole life that she was living, the one she'd built when she'd come back here pregnant.

It might not have been the one she'd planned, but it was a good one. She cleaned out some of the rental properties around town, because more seemed to pop up in their little community all the time, even in the winter. She'd talked to a few of the owners—because she knew them all—and got herself the gig.

Now, while the twins were in nursery school, she went and hit whatever units need a cleaning. Rosie wouldn't be jetting off to any fancy locations anytime soon, but cleaning allowed her to keep herself and her kids fed and clothed and not a burden on her family.

And, bonus, she liked cleaning. She did not have OCD, as Matilda claimed. Rosie liked the simple pleasure of setting things to rights.

She never really ran into members of the Carey family that much anyway. She didn't spend time in bars, where the single brothers often were. She wasn't a rancher. It had been a complete fluke that she'd been in the feed store when Zeke was that day.

As more time passed and she didn't see him, she relaxed.

Rosie began to think that maybe they would all just carry on as they were, and it was a relief. She told herself that it was the way things were supposed to be.

And Ryder wouldn't stay here. That wasn't who he was.

He was a problem that he would solve on his own, no need for her to get involved.

Then one day, right as February was getting ready to give itself over to the roaring March lion waiting in the wings, she picked the boys up in the afternoon the way she always did. She took them home, let them out to romp in the snow, and was unloading the groceries when a truck pulled up in front of the house.

And then everything happened much too fast.

Like a nightmare, Ryder Carey was standing right in front of her. Right there, in the front yard of the little house that she and Matilda lived in, tucked away on the hillside below the lodge.

"What the hell are you doing here?" she blurted out, making both Levi and Eli shriek with scandalized laughter, because they knew that she wasn't supposed to say *hell*. It was a bad word that only their naughty cousins said, as they always reported back with glee.

"I've been meaning to come over here and see you," Ryder said, very formally, and Rosie felt like she was having an out of body experience.

Because he was as beautiful as she remembered, maybe more so. And she'd never heard him sound *formal* before.

That night had been all about that slow, hot smile…

And this couldn't be happening. And the boys were *right here.*

"I owe you an apology," Ryder said. "I'm sure you've long since moved on, but my behavior that night was—"

Levi and Eli pushed in, each grabbing onto one of her legs, staring up at the strange man in the snowy front yard with great interest.

Then, the way he had last fall, Levi pointed straight at Ryder.

"Eyes," he said.

The exact same thing he'd said to Zeke.

Ryder looked down at both boys as if he'd forgotten they were there. Or was only just seeing them, and was modifying whatever words he'd been about to choose.

But he stopped dead.

His face went pale. He looked from Levi to Eli, then back again.

And when he looked back at Rosie, he had a completely different expression on his face.

Pale, yes. But lit through with pure fury.

"Rosie." His voice was colder than the afternoon around them, inching toward an icy dark. He said her name like it was the filthiest curse he could come up with, and she flinched, but she didn't look away. It was the least she could do. "Are they…?"

Her throat was so dry it hurt. "Ryder."

He looked… something far more deep and deadly hurt than *outraged*, but he was that, too. She could see it.

She could *feel* it.

Ryder took a step back. Then he surprised her by squatting down in front of the boys.

And ripped her heart out when he smiled at them, with a smile that matched the ones they offered him. First tentatively, then fully.

"Hey," Ryder said, in a tender voice she didn't know was possible, coming from a man who usually sounded like a hard shot of whiskey tasted. "How old are you guys?"

Eli smiled wider and stared. Levi puffed up his chest in his little parka. "We three in March," he said proudly. "That's older than two."

Rosie stood there, torn between begging Ryder not to do this *in front of her children* and knowing she had no say in how he took this in. She watched him do the math. She saw the way it hit him, like a hammer.

He smiled at the boys.

Then he stood again, his dark gaze like fire, and she felt it tear through her.

"You better start talking, Rosie," he said in a voice that was even worse than the way he looked at her. "And fast."

Chapter Three

"N O," ROSIE SAID, immediately.

And Ryder thought for a moment that he might actually spontaneously combust, right here and right now—

But she didn't look obstinate. She looked flustered. "I mean, of course. We will talk. We will. But not…"

She looked down at the two toddlers clinging to her legs, almost helplessly.

He could feel his blood pounding in every part of his body, and he'd felt something like this before. It felt a lot like getting tossed off the back of a nasty, mean-tempered bull at a terrible angle. And then, while hurtling through the air, he would have *just enough* time to wonder if this was the thing that was going to kill him. Snap his neck. Break every bone in his body.

Ryder felt like that now.

Like he was somewhere up in the air, waiting to see how he was going to land.

Only this was a lot worse than getting thrown.

He didn't know what to think. How to breathe. What to *do*.

Except follow her gaze down to those boys. Both of them were staring up at him, eyes wide with curiosity. Two little boys with dark blond hair and dark eyes, like red-cheeked memories in parkas and tiny snow boots.

Ryder didn't need any DNA tests to know whose kids these were. He *knew them* as if he could feel them in his own bones. He recognized them instantly. He'd spent his entire life looking at a face that had started out exactly like theirs, then turned into his. These boys looked so much like Wilder and Ryder as kids that it was uncanny. And in case he was tempted to question that, there were also old pictures of the two of them all over the ranch house.

He had been looking at a whole set of them last night, because he'd walked down that long hall with all the family photos on display on his way out.

There was no doubt about it. The two boys looking up at him could be Ryder and Wilder reincarnated.

Except he wasn't one of them. So that could only mean one thing.

He was a father. He was *their father*.

Everything had changed, right here on this hill that looked back down into the valley that was Cowboy Point. He could tell that his life whole life would forever hinge on his decision to swing by this house today. Everything would now be filed as *before* and *after* this moment.

This shocking understanding that he and Rosie had made babies that night.

And his pulse didn't slow down any, but he'd landed. Gotten his feet under him.

Ryder blew out a breath, aware of Rosie's pleading gaze on his. He squatted down, getting face-to-face with these twins—*his twins*—who made him feel like time travel had to be real.

He felt an overwhelming urge to simply... pick them up. To put his hands on them. To assure himself they were real. To take them away from here, from her, so he could learn every single thing there was to know about both of them. So he could catch up—

Another breath was necessary to keep himself even. Not *calm*, exactly, but in control.

"Gentlemen," he said, formally, looking from one pair of dark eyes just like his to the other. "I'm pleased to meet you."

He tipped his hat, then held out his hand, like his own father had taught him when he was about their age.

They stared at him. Then looked *delighted*.

"Boys, this is..." Rosie faltered. Cleared her throat. Ryder couldn't look at her. "Introduce yourselves."

"Eli," said the quieter of the two, the one who had seemed shy. He wasn't at all shy about sticking out his hand, and he looked nothing short of *delighted* when Ryder shook it.

Ryder found he felt the same way. Like there had been ice around his heart his whole life and he'd never known it until now, as it cracked wide open.

"I'm Levi," said the other little boy, shoving in to get his hand in Ryder's in place of his brother's. Then he looked up at his mother. "That's Mommy."

Ryder took his time shaking Levi's hand. Then Eli stuck his hand back in too so he was shaking both of their little hands, and they were both giggling so hard he couldn't help but smile. Then the two of them started speaking in what sounded like nonsense, but he figured it was their own, private language, a lot like the one Wilder and he had made up when they were little, too.

He didn't think about anything but the simple joy of it. The two of them so unaware of the way they'd changed the entire course of his life, as was only right and proper. The two of them so completely themselves, two happy little boys in snow clothes on a winter afternoon.

Two adorable twin boys and a brand-new father, shaking hands like men.

"Look," Levi shouted, turning away from the handshaking. "Uncle Wyatt!"

Ryder held onto Eli's little hand until he pulled away too, running after his brother. Only then did Ryder take his time rising back up to his feet.

He didn't look at Rosie. He couldn't. It all felt too raw.

But the sight greeting him on the road wasn't any better. Wyatt Stark had been a friend of his for as long as he could remember. The same went for the other two Stark boys—

who, like the so-called Carey boys, were all fully grown men now but rarely referred to that way—who piled out of the same truck at the edge of the yard.

He heard Rosie take a quick breath behind him, and glanced back despite himself to see that she looked nothing short of stricken.

Well, he thought. *Join the club.*

The twins went running toward their uncles and Ryder watched them go, with the strangest aching sensation in his chest as he watched how *comfortable* they all were. The ease with which those big, tough Stark brothers threw the little toddlers up in the air, passed them back and forth, and had them squealing with delight.

All things he'd imagined he would do, one day, when he was a father. Before reminding himself that he was never going to be a father.

No wonder it hit different today, now that he was one.

He glanced back at Rosie to find her eyes wide and filled with something like misery. Or maybe it was just plain old misery.

"Heard you were in town," Noah Stark said, drifting closer. "Keep thinking we'll see you in the Copper Mine now that your brother's abandoned us for the ball and chain lifestyle."

Noah was the youngest of the Stark brothers, and was roughly Ryder's youngest brother's age. The three Stark brothers lined up in age, more or less, with Ryder and

Wilder, Boone, and Knox. They'd caused a ruckus or two in their time, that was for sure.

But today was something else entirely. Ryder couldn't think of a thing to say, and the longer the silence dragged out, the more Noah narrowed his eyes suspiciously as he looked between Ryder and Rosie.

Ryder didn't have it in him to play this off. He just stood there, fully aware of the way his jaw was flexing, and stared the other man down.

Levi and Eli came running back again and careened into Ryder's legs this time. And Ryder got to watch as the three Stark brothers went through the same gamut of emotions that he had.

They looked at the boys.

They looked at Ryder.

They glared at Rosie.

"Rosie," Logan said in a low voice. "You don't really—"

"Why don't you take the boys up to the lodge," Rosie said, cutting him off. And though she forced a smile, it was clearly for the benefit of the boys because her gaze was anything but happy. "I'll text you in a little while."

"If you put a hand—" Wyatt began, with the bluster that had served him well in many an almost-barfight.

But Ryder was the one who'd taught him how to fight in middle school.

He cut his gaze toward the man he'd known all their lives, and let whatever expression was on his face do the talking.

Wyatt lifted his hands, palms up. He jerked his head at his brothers, and the younger two rounded up the twins. For a moment it was all the high-pitched, exciting chattering of the toddlers, then the truck engine starting up.

And then there was nothing but the kick of the wind on the mountains, that same wild drumming of his heart, and Rosie.

The woman who'd made him a father.

The woman who hadn't, as far as he could tell, ever intended to fill him in on the fact that they'd made themselves a couple of whole humans.

Rosie cleared her throat. Then again. "You'd better come in, Ryder."

She didn't make any eye contact as she turned back toward her car, but Ryder beat her to it. He told himself it was because he needed a task to focus on. It was better than focusing on this terrible sense of betrayal he felt. Besides, he'd had two mothers in his lifetime and they'd both taught him to mind his manners, no matter the circumstances.

He took the grocery sacks out of her arms, jerking his chin toward the front door of the house when she started to protest.

"Fine," she muttered, her cheeks looking red—redder than they would have anyway, having been outside in all this cold for this long. "Um. Thank you."

To calm himself, he forced himself to think about the

little house that she hurried toward. There was the lodge up on the top of this particular hill, standing there as a glamorous memory of a bygone age. And then, scattered all the way down to the valley floor were little cabins mixed in with slightly more expansive homes, like this one. They had all been built as outbuildings for the lodge in its heyday, as well as housing for the lodge's workers. He knew the Stark brothers lived in these houses, somewhere—and probably not all piled into the one he was pretty sure they'd commandeered at sixteen and had used to get up to all kinds of no good when they were all in high school. He was pretty sure someone had told him that Jack Stark now lived in the house on the lodge's grounds. Many of the cabins were short-term rentals these days, something he knew because he'd listened to his brother Knox, the youngest, lay out an entire retirement plan over Sunday dinner that involved short-term rentals and *building a portfolio* while the rest of them sat there experimenting to see which one of them could roll their eyes the hardest.

Big talk from a man who was MIA all morning today, Boone had said. Boone was built like a linebacker, or possibly a bear. He always looked like what he was, to Ryder's mind. Solid. Dependable. And perfectly capable of kicking some butt along the way.

You have to have a job to retire from it, Harlan had pointed-ed out. In that drawl of his that was as much a smack as a backhand would have been.

He thought about HGTV shows he'd watched while working through his endless physical therapy exercises, for maintenance these days rather than repair. He'd watched the home renovations. Real estate. Properties flipped and fancied up and sold.

It had always seemed like shell games within shell games to him.

By the time Rosie pushed her way to the front door that she apparently didn't keep locked—as he remembered it, no one locked anything this high up in the mountains, because why bother when there were so few people—he thought his blood pressure was back within manageable limits.

Inside, the tension rose again as the door swung shut and closed them in. But it was tempered somewhat by the fact that they had to stand there in the small foyer, shrugging out of their heavy coats, kicking off their boots, and adjusting to the heat indoors.

It was hard to keep the tension at its height when a man was padding across the living room floor in his socks.

Rosie didn't sit, so he didn't either. She stood there, closer to the door, like she wanted the option of bolting if necessary. Then she crossed her arms and looked at him as if she was waiting for him to roll out the nearest guillotine.

All those things he wanted to shout at her out there in the front yard, all of that disbelief and fury and something like betrayal, were… not exactly gone. But that roaring boil of too many feelings had calmed itself down into a simmer.

"What I need you to tell me," he said, as carefully as he could, "is—"

"They're yours," she snapped at him. "I realize you don't know this about me but I don't, in fact, get naked with every cowboy I meet."

"I know they're mine."

That came out a lot less careful. Their gazes slammed together, and that wasn't the greatest idea. Because her gaze was wide and that remarkable shade of blue. And he didn't need the word *naked* hanging there between them, either. He remembered her beneath him, gazing up at him, those too-blue eyes wide and glazed with heat and—

Rosie cleared her throat again. "Oh. Okay. I guess I thought the first thing you would ask me was to go get a blood test or something."

"Those little boys look exactly like Wilder and me when we were their age," Ryder said, forcing himself to keep his voice even, if not anything like *easy*. "I remember, but there are also pictures all over the house I grew up in. There are only two men in the entire world that could be their father, Rosie. And if a woman he'd slept with was suddenly walking around pregnant, then produced twins, Wilder would probably have some questions. So that leaves me, doesn't it?"

He watched as she stood a little straighter. Squared her shoulders. How she took her time doing it, like she, too, was trying to keep it smooth. Like she wanted to actually talk, not give into the heightened emotion that was pressing in on them in the small, tidy living room with windows that looked down the hill and into the valley.

And Ryder counted himself lucky to have known a whole lot of beautiful women in his time. So many that they sometimes seemed to blend together, and that was a shame. But this was the one that had haunted him.

This was the one that had really gotten to him, apparently, because after Rosie, it was always and only her face that he saw before him. Though he knew better than to say something like that, no matter how many unkind thoughts he might have been tempted to have about Rosie in that moment.

She was still gathering herself, so he did the same. Though what gathering himself looked like in this scenario was studying her.

Like she was a mystery that needed solving, and quick.

The most obvious thing about Rosie was that she looked exactly the same as his memory of her. That pretty gold and copper hair of hers that gleamed like summer even now, in the depths of February, was tucked back into something smooth and elegant. That perfect face, with a stubborn chin and the sort of mouth that made a man's imagination take over, was actually even more beautiful than his memories.

She had been dressed in jeans and cowboy boots down in Austin, with one of those strappy little tank tops for maximum distraction, and it had worked. Today, she was dressed for Montana cold, and that was never too fancy—though she was making a run at it. She was wearing jeans that did fantastic things to her bottom, but they also looked pristine. Not the least bit ratty or ripped or even stained. And the sweater she wore looked like one of those thin wool jobs, all about heat with none of the bulk, and he appreciated that, because he could see she was exactly as attractive as he remembered. Long legs. Wide hips. That indentation between them that he'd spent a lot of time appreciating that night, with a decent handful up top besides.

Rosie Stark was pretty. There was no getting away from that.

There was something else about her that he hadn't been able to define. Not that night and certainly not that morning after, when he'd been tempted to break his cardinal rule of one night only to see if maybe two nights might be even more fun—

But she'd woken up and looked at him with her heart in her eyes, and he'd reacted badly.

Now, under completely different circumstances, he could still see her heart in her eyes. Difference was, he now had a better idea of what it was about her that got to him.

It was that Stark stubbornness, very obvious to him now, as she made no attempt to explain herself. She simply stood there as if awaiting his judgment.

"I've been going over the reasons that I didn't tell you, and I still think they're all as valid as they were then," she said, after a good long while. Before he could react to that, she inclined her head a little. "I also don't think they're a good excuse."

That took a pretty decent swipe out of his outrage, and so Ryder listened as she laid it all out. Her thinking. Her notion of what he might do, should do, and hadn't. The fact that—valid or not—her life had felt like rolling heavy stones down a steep hill and at some points, it was all she could do to not get crushed.

He tried not to react, though he could feel the urge to respond, to fight, to argue, well up in him—

But this wasn't about him. He kept reminding himself of that. Whatever he felt—and he felt plenty—he would deal with. In the meantime, he had to think about those little boys. The sweet heartbreak when they'd gripped his hand, because they were *here* and they were *his* and he didn't know them at all.

And they didn't know he was their father.

Yet.

It didn't take a rocket scientist to figure out that shouting at their mother wasn't a smart way to go about gaining access to them. Ryder didn't question that he wanted that access, because it was already deeper than that.

He was a different man than the one who'd driven up here to offer a likely awkward apology to a woman he'd expected would have been happily married and moved on by now—and he didn't just *want* to know his kids. He *needed* to know them.

"That's how it happened," Rosie told him, when she came to a stop on a jagged sort of breath. She squared her shoulders again. "But I realized today, right outside in the driveway, that I've been kidding myself the whole time. The whole entire time, because if you knew with one look it was only a matter of time until everyone else did, too. It's been months since your father ran into us and I was so sure he knew too, immediately, but nothing happened so—"

Everything inside Ryder went very, very quiet. And still. "What did you just say?"

Rosie looked alarmed. "Didn't he tell you? I thought that's why you were here."

"He didn't tell me anything." Ryder had to fall back on the control that had kept him competing with minimal injuries all these years. "I came here to apologize. I was a dick that morning. You didn't deserve it. I've been carrying that around with me and I wanted to say so."

It was almost funny now, to think about how little his morning-after behavior mattered in the grand scheme of things. Now that there were two little lives in the mix. Though really, that was a pretty good reason not to come rushing to tell him, wasn't it?

"Thank you," Rosie replied. "You were a dick. But that hardly matters."

Then they stood there a while longer, on opposite sides of the cheerful little space, staring at each other.

Ryder had been treated to a great many out of body experiences in his lifetime. Pain could do that to a man. So could terrible defeats, unexpected victories, and pretty much everything in between. He'd wanted a life of *more* and he'd gotten it. More of everything meant… more of *everything*.

But this was something else.

He could remember with entirely too much detail how that night with Rosie had started. She'd found him at the meet and greet that night, pretty as a picture in a cowboy hat and a big grin.

Didn't expect to see a hometown girl in a place like this, he'd said, grinning, like the Moody Center was a den of iniquity instead of a world class arena.

I came to see the bulls, she'd replied. With that slow smile of hers aimed right at him and the sweet little pop of challenge in her gaze.

Well, Ryder had drawled, *I sure do hope I can drag your attention away. For seven seconds or so.*

He'd done better than that. He'd won the damned thing.

And he'd won the girl, too. Then he'd tossed her away, and hard, but they weren't here to discuss that. Yet what they were talking about was dangerous, because it had happened during all those glorious hours wrapped around each other in her pretty little apartment. Her roommates had been out of town.

She'd trusted him, because she knew him.

Ryder had sunk into her like he never meant to come up for air again.

There were two little boys running around because of that.

It wasn't like Ryder didn't know that sex led to babies. But knowing how something worked in theory and then living through it happening in practice wasn't the same thing.

"My family probably wouldn't have given you my cell phone number," he told her, instead of wading through too many feelings he couldn't quite name. "You would have had to tell them why you needed it, and who's to say they even would have believed it. Because it was you, maybe they would have. Over the years, there's been some weird stuff."

She blinked. "Okay."

"Not bragging here, Rosie. I'm telling you that it's unlikely they would have given you my cell phone number, and even if they did, I wouldn't have answered it. Two things can be true at once. I can recognize that you didn't have a lot of options and also be furious that there are two little boys that don't know that I'm their father."

"I guess I can't tell you not to be upset," she said, but she said it belligerently, to his ear. "But don't worry, Ryder. It's exhausting to be a parent. Taking care of two babies at once is no picnic, either. I'm lucky I had so much help, but you better believe that there were a lot of sleepless nights. And more tears than I can count. Mine, not theirs."

She didn't say that like she wanted sympathy, so he didn't offer it. "I know you're not saying that like you don't know that I couldn't possibly have helped you with that, because I didn't know it was happening."

"While we're throwing truths out on the table, why didn't you know?" she asked. "You were the one with all the experience. Everybody knows that Ryder Carey loves his buckle bunnies."

"I thought you were auditioning for the job."

She laughed at that, genuinely enough that he decided he regretted saying it.

"Oh, I was. Nothing could have been more unlikely, but I was going to have one night of fun and then get back to reality. But I guess the joke's on me, because it wasn't much fun, was it?"

"Are you going to stand here and tell me you didn't have a good time?" He could hear his voice drop. He could hear his own drawl. "Because that's not how I remember it. Time after time after time, what I remember is you seeing stars."

"Sure," she agreed. He didn't know when they'd come so close that they were standing just a whisper apart. "But so did you."

That felt like another terrific kick to the midsection, and it left him winded.

It made the room seem to spin, and the last time he'd felt that way in her presence, well. That had led to a pair of twins.

The twins. That was what he needed to concentrate on.

He moved away, tossing his hat aside and running a

hand through his hair.

"I don't need to litigate a one-night stand," he muttered.

"Maybe you should."

"I'll tell you what, Rosie," he began.

"By all means," she said in that snotty way of hers that he really should hate, and didn't, "tell me."

He couldn't hate her, not even now, and that was concerning. He wasn't happy with her, but that wasn't the same thing. He didn't know *this* was. What he did know was that driving over here, he'd been a little too excited about the prospect of seeing her again, and he didn't like to think what that might mean.

He focused on her. "You can bring out your big guns, scream yourself hoarse about the indignities you suffered that night. I support it. I came here to apologize for it. But how about we wait on that until we nail down a few other critical issues at hand."

She didn't like that. He thought there was little extra color in her cheeks as she folded her arms over her chest, but her voice was significantly less snotty when she spoke. "What do you want to nail down?"

"What do you think?" He frowned at her. "What's going to happen here, Rosie? The secret's out. Those are my kids."

"What does that mean to you?" And she laughed a little bit as she asked that, but he thought that sounded more hysterical than anything else. "How are you going to have custody of them if you're in a different city every weekend?

How would that work? Are you going to drag them from rodeo to rodeo? Get a babysitter?"

"That's how some folks do it."

"You mean that's how some families do it," she corrected him. "But we're not a family. So forgive me, but I'm not exactly in a hurry to hand my babies off to someone who, let's be honest, I don't know at all."

It was his turn to not like the turn of the conversation. "You know me well enough."

"I know stories about you from growing up. I know how you smile when you're flirting. I know you get mean when things get intense." Rosie lifted a shoulder, then dropped it. "So, you're right. I do know you. That's not exactly working in your favor when it comes to my babies. *My babies*," she repeated, in case he didn't get it. "I'm not denying that you're their father, but they don't know you."

"Whose fault is that?"

"That doesn't matter either." She slashed a hand through the air when he started to argue that. "What matters—the only thing I can let matter now, in fact—is that. I didn't mean for this to happen. Kind of like I'm betting you didn't mean to get me pregnant in the first place. But here we are."

"Don't absolve yourself too quickly, darlin'," Ryder suggested, and told himself the heat in him was temper. Not memories.

"Rule number one," she shot back. "Don't call me *dar-lin'*. You think I don't know that's the name you use when you can't remember the name of the girl you're with?"

"I always knew your name."

"Right. That's the hometown advantage, I guess?" She glared at him. "Don't start mixing me up with someone else now, please."

"That's unlikely, Rosie," he said, emphasizing her name. "Because as far as I know, you're the only baby mama I have."

"Rule number two," she continued, her voice stern. "The boys come first. That's the beginning and the end of everything. I mean it," she added, because he must have made some noise or something in response.

"You're laying down rules and I don't know anything about my own children," he said, after allowing himself a beat or two to simmer down a little. To remember that passion was what had caused this in the first place, so no need to let temper do the same. "You're going to have to give it a little space, Rosie. And thank you for thinking I'm some kind of monster. I'm not going to rip them away from you." He held her gaze. "I would never do that."

He remembered being a little kid when his mother died. When he and his brother made it all worse, though that was a different core memory that didn't need excavating just now. And he remembered when Zeke had first told him about Belinda, and how they'd all been afraid—even Harlan, who in those days had liked to act as if he was never afraid of anything—that she would be the kind of wicked stepmother they'd heard about in books and movies.

But she'd been Belinda instead. She was no replacement for Ryder's mother and had never tried to be. What she was, in every conceivable way, was a beautiful addition.

He'd met too many others, out on the tour, who'd had more typical stepparent experiences.

Ryder knew all about broken homes. They couldn't do anything about what had happened so far, but from this point forward, that was not going to be what happened to his boys. They might have two homes, but he by God was going to see to it personally that they were both happy.

"I don't know what you're going to do," Rosie said, mulishly, to his ear. "I also think that you don't know, either. We're still in the heat of the moment. Things could change. One thing that won't change, though, is that this is the only home those boys have ever known. I am the only parent that they've ever known. I'm not saying that's right or wrong, that's just how it is. That's what we need to be careful with as we proceed."

"So tell me how we'll be proceeding, then," he said. Maybe he was daring her. "Tell me how it's going to work?"

"It will work in baby steps," she replied, her brow wrinkling.

"Bullshit."

The furrow between her brows became a full frown. "What?"

"That's bullshit. You had years of baby steps, Rosie. I

don't want to overwhelm them. I don't know what the hell I want, if you want to know the truth. But I'll tell you this. I've known that I was a father for less than an hour and I'm already determined I'm going to be a good one. Whatever that looks like. And you don't get to decide how that happens, all on your own. You've already done enough of that."

He felt something like winded, but he meant every word he'd said. She looked like she wanted to argue, but instead she moved, jerkily. It was almost as if she was thinking about sitting down on the sofa, but decided to pace instead, and there was something comforting about that.

If he had to feel this agitated, he was glad she did too.

"They are funny, sweet, impossible, magical little boys," she told him, and her voice sounded something like urgent. "Levi is bossier. Eli is dreamier. But they're both wildly stubborn. And they're a unit. They don't like to do things without each other. I used to dress them differently when they were little, partly because it helped in telling them apart, and also partly because some people suggested that's what I *should* do."

"What people?"

Her cheeks flushed a deeper shade of red. "Books. Lots of books. I read that it was good to present twins with autonomy. But the funny thing is, now that they throw fits to wear what they want to wear, they prefer to dress alike. Maybe autonomy will come down the road, but as for now, what they like is being twins."

Ryder also liked being a twin. Their family had been sprawling and loud, with a lot of chaos and shifting alliances as everyone tried to do their thing in such a big crowd. But what Ryder and Wilder had always seen as the best stroke of luck imaginable was that they had each other. Sometimes they operated as a voting block. Sometimes they employed a little two on one to shift matters in their favor. They were a team.

But it was more than that. Having a twin had always meant, to Ryder, that there was just... more of him walking around. He and Wilder were connected in ways that Ryder didn't try to make any sense of.

It was just how it was. The two of them were never out of touch. They texted all day every day, and called each other a fair amount too, because they didn't catch each other up on the big events in their lives. They shared every last detail of their lives, so the big events seemed like *theirs*, not his or Wilder's individually. Another shared experience.

He didn't know how to explain this to Rosie.

"Of course they like being twins," he said instead. "Particularly identical twins. Fraternal ones got shafted. Some of the fun, fewer of the benefits."

She was still pacing and he looked past her to the fireplace. And new things seem to bloom just to twist up inside of him. He walked that way, and probably should have noticed the way her eyes widened, as if she thought—

But no, he thought piously, *that isn't what's happening*

here.

He reached past her and picked up one of the framed picture that sat on the mantel. It was of two toothy little chunks in baby clothes, all round faces, bright and happy with wet smiles.

That things inside him twisted, hard.

Ryder found himself running a hand over his face and for a moment that stretched out much too long, he wasn't entirely sure that he wouldn't do something that he'd regret later. Like puke out his guts. Or worse, double over in the face of all these things he felt inside.

Instead, he put the picture back, very carefully. He scanned the rest of them, documenting two very short, very cute lives that he'd missed so far. When he turned to look at her, she was staring at him with that stricken expression on her face once more.

"Ryder," she began.

"Why don't we start with some pictures," he said, cutting her off, his voice hoarse. "I want to see what I missed."

Chapter Four

LATER THAT NIGHT, Ryder found Zeke in the small tack room he used in the barn. Once it had been for farm use, then it was an office, but now it was Zeke's workshop. It was where he made his spurs and his bits these days so he could sell them in the summer market and online.

Ryder was happy that he was there, and alone.

He wasn't quite ready to go wide to the whole family about the day he'd had and how everything had changed. In an instant.

Though he did pause in the doorway to take a look at the old man.

For the second time today, he looked at someone else and saw himself, but this time in the other direction. It made him feel about as close to dizzy as he'd ever been without a head injury. Those tiny, new faces that were the way his had been. This old, weathered face that was the way his was heading.

The driving force that had led him here tonight, the snow be damned, kicked in again.

Harder than before.

"You knew that Rosie Stark had my babies and didn't

tell me," he said, shoving his way in through the door.

He hadn't forgotten that she'd told him that, though there had been other things to focus on in the moment. It had been one more drum beating inside of him the whole of the night, and it got almost too loud to bear as he navigated a slippery path through the snowstorm that had blown in when he finally headed home.

After he'd had dinner with *his children* for the first time. After he'd watched Rosie be a mother, making them dinner and arguing them in and out of the bathtub. Reading them stories, then tucking them into bed.

Do you live here? Levi had asked while they were snuggling into the bed they still wanted to share, in a small bedroom with horses and trucks all over the walls.

I don't, Ryder had told him.

Ryder is your daddy, Rosie had said, very matter-of-factly, with only a sideways look at Ryder to indicate that she knew this was a huge thing, this acknowledgment.

He'd actually held his breath as he'd waited for the boys to respond.

Jacinta has a daddy, Eli had said, like that settled the matter.

Rosie had bitten back a smile as she'd informed Ryder that Jacinta was Eli's best friend at nursery school.

Is he my daddy too? Levi had asked in a stage whisper.

I'm both your daddy, Ryder had said then. *And it's past your bedtime.*

If he'd found himself sweating from a performance far more precarious than any he'd given before, he certainly didn't want anyone to see it. Just like he didn't want to tell anyone—because he didn't know how to feel about it—that the act of tucking the boys in and leaving them in their bed, sleepy and safe, made his heart actually, physically hurt in his chest.

Rosie had walked him out. They had said very little. Everything was too big, maybe. The ramifications were still coming at them, fast, and she probably knew as well as he did that the reckoning was only just beginning.

That Ryder Carey had knocked up Rosie Stark and left her on her own for a couple of years was going to take some digesting, and not just on his part.

Whatever it was, all he'd done was nod at her, stiffly, and then take himself home. He'd been glad it was dark and cold. He'd been glad that he'd had to focus on the road to make sure he didn't slide off and over the side of the mountain.

He'd driven in total silence, save that drumbeat inside of him. It had gotten deafening by the time he made it to the ranch. He'd driven past the turnoff to his and Wilder's plots and straight on to the house, where he could see the lights on inside.

If they hadn't also been on in the barn, he would have turned around, gone back to his Airstream, and looked for answers in a bottle of whiskey. They were never there, those elusive answers, but a complicated life meant a man kept looking.

Zeke glanced up from what he was doing with a mild expression on his face.

"You're not going to lie to me, are you?" Ryder asked incredulously.

"I've been many things in this life," his father said in that slow drawl of his that always made Ryder stand a little bit straighter, like he was still a kid. "But a liar has never been one of them."

"How could you keep something like that to yourself?"

"I thought about telling you." Zeke turned his attention back to the metal in his hands. "But we're talking about two boys' lives, Ryder. You made it very clear that bull riding comes first. Above and before every other thing in your life. Why add to that list?"

"That's fucked up and you know it."

Again, Zeke seemed profoundly unbothered. Maybe *too* unbothered, though Ryder couldn't think why that was.

"Children aren't a game," his father told him. "You can't pick them up and put them down when you're bored."

That seemed profoundly unfair, given Ryder had known he was a parent for only a handful of hours.

"I didn't ask you for parenting lessons," he gritted out. "I want to know why you knew something of critical importance to my life and chose to keep it to yourself."

Zeke looked up at him then, and while he didn't look

unbothered anymore, he didn't look apologetic, either. "What would you have done?"

Ryder stared back at him, aware that every muscle in his body was tense. Particularly his jaw, which felt soldered shut.

"What would you have done?" Zeke asked again, as if he was being gentle and reasonable when Ryder would have preferred a punch in the mouth. "If I called you, back in the fall, would you have packed up everything you own and hurried home? And if you had, would you have come here to make Rosie's life easier or harder?"

Again, and not for the first time today, Ryder felt winded.

"I'm your son," he managed to get out.

"You are. And Rosie Stark is a good girl. She's been through a lot in this town."

He didn't add *alone*, but it lingered there, like an accusation made into another piece of metal for his father to use as he pleased.

"Dad, I don't know how to break this to you, but you're supposed to support your own family first."

"And in public, that is what I will always do," Zeke told him staunchly. "Even in private. You know that I'll always support you. You're my son and I love you. But between you and me, Ryder. Man to man? Well. That's a different story. I can support you and also not do what you think I should."

Ryder had always wondered if a man knew he was having a heart attack before it happened. Now he wondered if it happened like this, his own heart beating so hard and so intently in his chest that it felt like he was clobbering himself from the inside out.

"So you think she was right to hide the existence of my children from me for years. Is that what you're telling me?"

"I didn't say that." Zeke kept his gaze level on Ryder's. "But I can understand why she did it. Can't you?"

And the thing was, Ryder really could understand it. He'd told Rosie that much himself.

But he sure didn't like hearing it from his own father, dying or not.

Though Zeke had sure seemed healthy as a horse while doling out the kill shots tonight. No frailty or blanket around the shoulders in sight.

Ryder threw himself back outside to find the snow had stopped. His breath made clouds against the night sky. His heart was a percussion section. He felt as if something was holding him in a tight grip, and squeezing him more by the second.

He glared back at the barn and the obstinate father who certainly seemed healthy enough to be throwing zingers, getting in some metalworking, and casting aspersions on his own flesh and blood.

This homecoming thing was getting more complicated by the moment.

He got in his truck and drove back down the hill, but instead of turning up Wilder's drive, he took the other drive toward his own little plot.

It took some doing. No one had driven down that way since the snow had started coming down in the fall. Ryder had a bit of a time making sure he stayed on what ought to be the road, instead of skidding off into the trees.

When he got there, the plot was still cleared, because that's what he and Wilder had done with both of their bits of land as soon as they'd got them. They'd cleared them off together, talking big games about what they'd do with them, and then… hadn't.

Or anyway, Ryder hadn't. Wilder had built his first cabin the summer after high school. Then he'd added to it and updated it throughout the years.

Ryder had taken all the savings he'd ever had and had made the down payments on his truck and his Airstream. Then he'd left, heading straight for whatever rodeo would have him.

Tonight he parked his truck in the general area of where a cabin would sit, if he ever got around to building one. He hadn't thought about settling down like that, not in a long time. Maybe not ever, not really.

But all he could think about tonight were the faces of those little boys. *His* little boys. Levi and Eli, names that almost rhymed but didn't, just like him and Wilder. He'd spent most of the night staring at the two of them, trying to figure out if he thought they favored Rosie more, or him. Every time he thought he had the answer, he changed his mind again the next moment.

They were as different as they were alike, two silly, funny, happy little boys.

Tempting as it was to sit here and get dark and grim about all the things that had been kept from him, and he could certainly go that route—he could see the entrance yawning at him from afar—he had to factor in the inarguable fact that Rosie was doing a good job with them.

That was no small thing. Ryder hadn't had to leave Montana—or even Cowboy Point—to understand that parents didn't always do the best job with their kids. Especially not when they were on their own. He'd certainly gotten a broader view of that kind of thing as he'd traveled around the country again and again.

His sons—and something in him seemed to sputter to a halt, then pound back to life at the thought of it. *His sons.* He swallowed, hard.

They were well cared for. They were happy. They had family, a roof over their heads, a mother who adored them, and he couldn't find fault in any of it.

That didn't mean he was happy about it.

Maybe there was no getting himself happy about it.

Because what Zeke had said to him was settling in, like its own kind of ache. He still thought his father was wrong to not have told him—but what *would* he have done? What would he have done if Rosie had come and found him as soon as she'd learned she was pregnant?

Here, now, it was easy to puff up and claim that *obviously* he would have done the right thing, whatever that looked like for Rosie—but would he have?

Ryder knew himself pretty well and he doubted it.

And that sad, selfish truth sat in him like indigestion, making it hurt to breathe.

He sat there a long time. And he might have sat there longer still, but he was interrupted from his contemplation of the darkness before him, the suggestion of mountains in the distance, and the outlines against the night sky by a set of headlights coming down the track he'd made in the snow.

He braced himself for Wilder, but it was Boone's truck that pulled into view, and then bumped its way right up next to his. Boone looked over at him, then climbed out of his own truck and came around to swing himself into Ryder's passenger seat.

"I saw lights where there shouldn't have been any lights," Boone said with a grunt as he settled, the blast of cold air from outside swirling around them both. "Had to come see what was happening over here."

"What did you think was happening?" Ryder asked, genuinely curious. It was after midnight on a very cold night after another snowstorm. It was a typical February night in Montana and smart people were tucked up indoors, as close to a heat source as possible.

"Could be poachers," Boone said, in that deadpan way of his, as if there was a rash of poaching exploits in the dead of winter. Or ever, because this was Montana, where everyone was armed.

Besides, there was nothing to poach in this snowy clearing.

The brothers sat there a while, contemplating the night.

"What are you doing wandering around so late?" Ryder asked. Eventually.

Boone shrugged, a rustle of his heavy jacket. "I was down at Sierra's. Something going on with her generator and there's a whole lot of winter to get through yet."

Ryder considered that. "And her husband's not around to handle that sort of thing?"

He figured that he'd kept his tone sufficiently neutral when it came to the contentious topic of Boone's lifelong female best friend, because Boone actually answered. "Business trip."

If Ryder was any other one of his brothers, he would have jumped on that. He would have pointed out that no husband worth his salt would ever have tolerated the relationship that Boone had with Sierra. And no, he didn't reckon that Sierra's husband was simply more highly evolved or trusted his wife or any of the other things Boone had said over the years to make it seem like anyone asking was deeply immature.

It was pretty clear to Ryder that he didn't care.

He could have said all of that, but he didn't. He had his own problems.

Problems that the entire community of Cowboy Point was going to know all about, likely by morning. Assuming they didn't already know, thanks to the Stark brothers.

He saw no reason to give Boone a preview.

Besides, he still had no idea what he was going to say once the parentage of Rosie's twins was public knowledge. The twins themselves had accepted that he was their daddy and that was all that *really* mattered, he decided.

"I need to get over and see what you're doing with that dairy," he said instead. "Though I'll be honest, I don't know how to feel about the fact that folks around here are signing up for an *artisan milkman*."

"If it wasn't me I would hate me," Boone agreed with his big, booming laugh. "That was Sierra's idea. She lives down in Marietta and has a first-row seat to the kind of crafty, artistic takes on regular things that people are drawn to these days. Everyone wants small, local, and accessible. They want to meet the cow that made their milk and their cheese, and if it could come in a pretty package? Even better."

"Please tell me you do not have meet and greets with your herd."

Boone looked over at Ryder. "Oh, it's on now. This summer? I'm making the herd a tourist attraction. I might give them their own social media account. Just wait."

Ryder couldn't engage with the idea of social media cow accounts, which he had a sneaking suspicion probably already existed. "A tourist attraction. Here."

"The dairy is all the way over on the other side of the creek," Boone said with a laugh. "Mom made it pretty clear that she didn't want to wake up of a morning with a dairy smell coming in her windows. But I guarantee you, she'll be all over it when the weather's nice and the city people come down from Bozeman to cosplay the farming life for a week or so."

Ryder tried to imagine Belinda mucking around with the cows. Not that she wouldn't. He'd never seen his stepmother balk at a thing. But everyone was older now, and with four large, strapping men around to handle things—five, he amended, since he was technically here right now—why should she continue doing anything that looked like labor? He doubted he was the only one who thought she absolutely should not.

"I'm amazed that you even came up with an idea like this," he said. "I thought the point of the ranch was to do the same thing that's always been done, except more so, forever."

Boone slid him a look at that, but didn't comment. "A man likes to do something that's his. Besides, one night I was running my mouth about exactly that and Sierra dared me to actually do something about it. So I did."

He laughed, like he'd told himself a joke. Once again, Ryder didn't comment, though he was fascinated by every part of that story. The idea of Boone, a man who preferred to let his actions speak, running his mouth at all took some imagining. And then, again, there was the Sierra factor. The *best friend* thing, when Boone had obviously been in love with her his entire life.

But Ryder was hardly in a position to comment on anyone else's messy life.

Soon after, when Boone got back in his own truck and drove away, Ryder meant to follow him. Really he did.

Yet instead, he stayed where he was. Maybe it turned out that he liked the view here a lot more than he'd ever thought he would when there was so much world yet to see. There was something about this particular clearing, the specific arrangement of mountains and hills and Cowboy Point in the distance, and the trees that stretched up around him.

For the first time in as long as he could remember, the thought of settling down in a place like this didn't fill him with that terrible itchiness. That restlessness that snuck beneath his skin, sunk into his bones, and agitated him until everything in him demanded his escape.

He hadn't felt like that in the week or so he'd been home. That made it something like a record. Usually he was ready to walk to the nearest airport within twelve hours. Maybe he'd been changing even before he saw a whole new world in two pairs of curious dark eyes.

The only place he went tonight was back up the snowy drive. He eased his truck into the other road that forked off and led down around to Wilder's house.

He turned his lights off before he came out of the trees, because he didn't want to disturb Wilder and Cat. He made sure the door to his Airstream didn't slam shut.

Once inside, he marched to the back bedroom, crawled into his bed, and lay there. He stared up at his ceiling, sure that he would fall asleep at any moment.

But he didn't.

Instead, he found himself going over every single moment of that night in Austin, and by the time he finally slept, it seemed to be for no other purpose than to slide out of memory and into dreams of the same thing.

Rosie. Always Rosie.

When he finally got up the next day, he'd slept most of the morning away. There was an insistent sort of snow coming down, crafted specifically to build up the snowpack, not to adorn anything or make it pretty.

He messed around in his kitchen until he got the coffee going, then looked out his windows and saw that there were a number of trucks parked outside Wilder's house. His brothers' trucks. And he had the feeling that he was looking at an intervention, so he decided he didn't need any part of that. He wasn't ready to defend himself.

And he certainly wasn't ready to let Rosie be the topic of conversation. Or her boys.

Our boys, he corrected himself.

Instead, he threw on some clothes, went out to his truck, and headed down into Cowboy Point, ignoring the gathering at Wilder's completely.

He heard his phone buzzing, but ignored that too.

Without even meaning to, at least not consciously, he didn't take the road all the way down into town. Instead, on the crest of that hill where the old lodge stood he turned off winding his way into the trees until the road looped him around to Rosie's house.

When he knocked on the door, she answered, already frowning at him.

"They're napping." Her voice was short. He didn't like it. "You can't just show up here, Ryder."

"You could maybe ratchet back on that tone of voice that suggests I show up here all the time, out of the blue, when you and I both know that's not the case."

"You literally showed up yesterday. Out of the blue."

"You've known that you're a parent for a lot longer than I have, Rosie," he said then, in a low voice. Her expression changed, so he continued. "That's not me blaming you for that. That's me asking you for a little slack while I figure this out."

She blew out a breath. "I've been thinking a lot about this since you left last night. Obviously. And I think that there's no reason we can't be civilized about it. If we both commit to putting the boys first, I don't see why we can't come to a mutual agreement on the best way forward."

There was nothing inherently wrong with what she'd said. And yet he still didn't like it.

Maybe because he wasn't feeling anything like reasonable right now, standing on her front step with snow coming down on the both of them.

"Rosie." His voice sounded deep and urgent, but he couldn't change it when he heard it. It was the only tone that fit. "Twenty-four hours ago, I didn't know that we made anything that night but memories. I had no idea I had one child, much less two. You want to sit here and talk visitation rights and custody battles and whatever else? I'm not there yet. I'm still trying to understand how the hell I'm supposed to turn myself into a father overnight. Meanwhile, I think you and I both know there's no possible way your cousins didn't tell everyone in town."

She bristled at that, just a little, but he saw it.

"They're mine," she said. "Same way they've always been. Nothing to talk about."

"Sure," he said. "Except the part where you've made sure that I'll always be known as a deadbeat dad."

She opened her mouth and then shut it again.

Ryder took that as reluctant agreement. "I'm starting off behind, that's all I'm saying. Explain to me how you think I should go from not having the slightest idea that those boys exist to worrying about being *civilized* in less than a day. Do you think you could do that? Because I have to say, I don't think I'm being unreasonable that I'm finding this a little... That I'm finding this *a lot*."

He said all of that a little too quickly, maybe. A little too intently. It was the best he could do with all the competing storms crashing around inside of him.

Then he braced himself, because he really thought she was going to blow up at him, but she didn't.

Something changed in her face. Her eyes softened. She looked at him like she was trying to take him in for a long moment, then away.

He couldn't tell what she was looking at. The snow. The hills. The whisps of smoke from other people's chimneys that made the air smell rich and woodsy.

When she looked back she seemed to see too much of him. But instead of backing away, she gave him a jerky sort of nod.

"You better come inside," she said quietly, like there was the same sense of something like inevitability, or fate, heavy in her chest, too.

Then she opened the door wider and let him in.

Chapter Five

"SO NOW THAT we've all gotten past the *oh my God* part and the *how did I not see this from the beginning* part," Matilda said one evening in the early part of March, "can we go back to the *you've seen Ryder Carey* naked part?"

Rosie froze, her fork halfway up toward her mouth.

They were sitting in their brother Jack's house, which had once been the caretaker's house up on the top of the hill, next to the lodge. Maybe it was still the caretaker's house, given that Jack was the one leading the slow and steady charge to restore the old lodge and open it again. Tonight Rosie was just glad that there were no parents, grandparents, or other historic personages of note around to hear *that* come out of Matilda's mouth. And thank goodness the boys were in the other room, completely entranced by one of the cartoons they loved.

Matilda was smiling innocently at Rosie from across the table. For his part, Jack looked like he would love nothing more than to walk out the back door and fling himself off the nearest mountain.

Rosie felt the same.

"Matilda," Jack said in that disappointed voice of his. "I

am trying to eat my dinner."

Matilda waved a dismissive hand. "He's a remarkably good-looking man, Jack. I'm sorry for you that you can't see that. Truly I am."

"I'm aware that he's not a troll," Jack said with a sigh. "But I'm also aware that the topic is probably a sensitive subject around here."

Then Jack and Matilda set about exchanging *important looks, hefty with meaning*, as if Rosie was so fragile that a simple mention of Ryder's name might shatter her into pieces where she sat.

When surely if that was going to happen, it would have happened already.

She lowered her fork and stabbed it into the heap of buttery spaghetti smothered in Jack's signature sauce in front of her, so violently she made herself smile.

"Thank you for this frankly unnerving show of sympathy," she said, smiling tightly at Jack. "But of all the people sitting at this table, I'm the one who's always known the truth about Ryder Carey. And no, Matilda, I don't mean his pectoral muscles."

Though they were splendid, as she recalled.

"I bet they're amazing," her sister muttered, making Rosie wonder if Matilda could read the truth about Ryder's truly stunning physique on Rosie's face, and if she could... could everyone? Could Jack? The very idea made her want to cringe off into the snow. "And to think. There's *two* of him."

Rosie kept her smile welded onto her face. It was one of the greatest accomplishments of her college career. Because here's what she'd learned in her sorority at UT. The more she smiled, the more people *believed* that smile, and it didn't matter if she was screaming on the inside.

"There's been a lot of talk about the situation," Jack said gruffly, returning his attention to his food. "You know how folks like to talk around here. How are you holding up?"

"I'm used to a lot of talk," Rosie assured him. "What you find out when you show up pregnant in the tiny little town where you grew up, but with no husband or explanation, is that a lot of the people in it aren't quite as nice as you used to think."

"That just makes me furious." This wasn't the first time Matilda had expressed such sentiments. She'd been outraged on Rosie's behalf from the start. Once she'd even 'accidentally' let an overly fed cattle dog she'd rescued bound out of her cute red pickup to bowl over Gwen Sheen, the daughter of the owners of the feed store, as she stood on the sidewalk talking smack about Rosie. Matilda didn't play, people only thought she did. "What business is it of anybody else's anyway?"

"On the other hand," Rosie continued, "other people come out of nowhere and are wonderful. You just never know what you're going to get. So no, I'm not worried about people talking about Ryder and me. The boys are too young to understand, and from their perspective, they have a new friend who plays with them all the time and that they get to call Daddy. It's a win-win."

This was all true. Ever since Ryder had appeared at her doorstep, both the first and the second time, she had been scrupulous in separating out the things she felt allowed to feel—because it supported the boys and what they needed—and the things that were hers. The private things that only she knew.

The things that kept her up at night, mixing memory with fantasy, and driving herself wild.

That part was hard enough to deal with every night. It certainly wasn't something she intended to discuss in the presence of her older brother.

Also, and more importantly, she meant it about the surprising support from other people.

Take, for example, Kendall Carey and Cat Lisle—though, she corrected herself, she was pretty sure Cat went by Cat Carey now, not that it mattered in Cowboy Point where she would forever be a Lisle. Rosie had seen the two of them at Mountain Mama one chilly afternoon. Rosie had been stopping in to pick up one of their handmade half-baked pizzas for dinner before she swung by to pick up the boys. Cat and Kendall had been there, sitting close together in the corner, making each other laugh. A lot.

Rosie had expected that when they met eyes, they would all nod politely, and pretend not to know each other. That was how folks rolled in a tiny little mountain town in winter, when it was only the locals around, Mountain Mama was pretty much the only restaurant in the community that was open all the time, and every hello came with the risk of an in-depth conversation about everyone's business, and their parents' business, and each and every one of their cousins' business too.

Selective blindness was a necessity around here.

But the opposite happened. Kendall waved when she saw Rosie. And when Rosie only blinked at her in confusion—and likely some alarm—she got to her feet, came over, and tugged Rosie with her back to that table.

We've been wanting to talk with you, Cat had said when they got there. *And here you are. It's like fate.*

It's like a small town, Rosie had replied.

Cat and I like to get away every now and again, Kendall had carried on, as if Rosie hadn't said something deliberately grumpy. *Just the two of us.*

Because only the two of us have the exquisite pleasure of knowing entirely too much about the inner workings of the Carey brothers. Cat had smiled at Rosie. *And you are the only other person in town who could join that club.*

Rosie reacted so strangely that even now, thinking back on it, she hardly knew what to make of it. For one thing, those words went through her like an electric shock. A deep, chaotic, endless *humming*, deep and long.

And she was pretty sure that she blushed hot and red.

Oh no, she'd said at once. *I can't be in your club.*

More of a support group, Cat had replied with a grin.

In case the rumor mill hasn't gotten around to you yet with the full story, Ryder and I did not have a relationship, Rosie had told them. *That is not the word used to describe what happened between us.*

There were other words. She thought about those other words all the time, but that was inappropriate for an early afternoon discussion in a family-friendly joint like this.

You have the most intimate relationship that anyone could have with a man, Kendall corrected her, gently enough, but with enough intensity that Rosie found herself surreptitiously looking to see if Kendall looked like she was getting rounder. Looking wasn't rude, asking was rude, she assured herself, but her quick sweep was inconclusive. *You're the mother of his children. It doesn't matter if you spent fifteen minutes with him. That was then. Now you're going to be part of his life forever.*

That had definitely sounded like something a pregnant woman would say.

That makes you one of us, Cat had chimed in, smiling so wide and so happy that Rosie knew she had to *do something* to stop whatever runaway train this was.

Maybe Kendall had seen that on her face. *It's okay if you're not the joining type.*

What we really wanted you to know, Cat had said then, in the same tone, *is that we've got your back.*

Apparently, Kendall said with a smile, *Careys stick together.*

I'm not a Carey, Rosie had gritted out, and there was no reason why a simple statement of fact should have been so hard for her to say. She shouldn't have felt as if she was tearing out her own throat in an effort to save it.

Your sons are Careys, Cat had pointed out. Gently enough. *So I'm sorry, but you're kind of one too. By default.*

Rosie had never been more relieved to hear her name called by Indy Bennett up at the counter, giving her the perfect excuse to get the hell away from the two of them. She could appreciate the gesture, she told herself as she hurried out to her car, meeting no more eyes. She could appreciate it, but it was misplaced.

Later, she watched her boys roughhouse in the small aisles of the general store while she picked up a few essentials and was very aware of all the eyes on the two of them. And on her.

It had been like that for weeks. Just as Ryder had predicted.

The difference this time around was that when Nevaeh Higgins saw her, she didn't charge right over to share whatever word the Lord had put on her heart. Something that had happened with alarming regularity before, since Nevaeh was the pastor's wife. These days, however, Nevaeh only looked at Rosie sadly, as if the Lord himself didn't have anything to say when there was a Carey brother involved.

Maybe she needed a little support group after all.

She didn't feel like that was something she needed to tell Jack.

After dinner, Matilda started playing an involved game of tag with the little ones and Rosie knew what was coming when Jack came and sat with her on the sofa. He favored low-slung, comfortable leather, and she liked to sink into it. His house was decidedly male, with an emphasis on dark woods, dark walls, and what she could only describe as Montana-style furnishings.

Except unlike the short-term rentals she worked in, she knew that the buck on the wall was one Jack had shot himself.

Authenticity was important.

But her brother had gotten his steel-gray eyes from their father, who had been famously harsh. Jack knew exactly how to use them to his best advantage, and he was training them on her now.

"Here's the thing," he said quietly, looking at the beer in his hand, not her. "You know that I support you no matter what. I support you. I love you. I would do anything for you and those boys."

"This is sounding more ominous by the moment."

"It was unfair, the way people treated you when you came home. I never liked it. This isn't the 1800s. They never dared say those things to me, and that just made it worse, in my opinion."

Rosie actually smiled at that. "It's *almost* like people are sexist."

"The thing is, I can't understand is why you kept Ryder's

involvement a secret," Jack said, and those steel gray eyes seemed to pierce her straight through. He lifted a hand before she could reply. "I'm not asking you what happened between the two of you. I am fully aware that a man can seem one way in his everyday life, and still treat women terribly in private."

It made Rosie want to throw up, but she couldn't let that pass. "He didn't treat me horribly," she gritted out. "Not the way you mean. Is this really something you want to talk about?"

"Not at all." Jack swore under his breath. "But this is the thing, Rosie. You moved back here. You settled in, had the babies, and stayed. Don't get me wrong, I'm happy you did. But you must have known that sooner or later, someone was going to realize that those twins are the spitting image of their daddy. And their daddy is well-known here."

"Everyone who lives here is well-known here," she managed to say, though her throat was tight.

Jack continued to stare straight into her with all that steely gray. "Some might argue that he's the least known of the Carey brothers, but here's what folks do know. He's not a monster. Even if he was, his entire family is here, and everyone knows that Zeke Carey wants nothing more than a few grandchildren. It's hard to understand why you kept this to yourself all this time."

Rosie blew out a sigh. "I don't know."

Jack only looked *more* disappointed in her, then. "Come

on, Rosie."

"It seemed wrong to tell other people when I hadn't told Ryder. And I couldn't find him to tell him." She felt all the old *grossness* of it bubbling up inside her. "I couldn't think of a good enough reason to ask one of his brothers for his number. Much less his *dad*. And then somehow, in the middle of all that, they're about to turn three. I didn't mean to keep a secret. Mostly I was thinking about keeping me, and then them, safe. And, you know, *alive*."

"Matilda says he's been taking an interest these last couple weeks."

"More than an interest. I think that if he could, he would move in so he could be with them night and day." Rosie swallowed, but it was hard. "And I can't blame him. I feel the same way about them."

"Because you know that's not how they're spinning it in town," Jack told her, his voice going stern and that beer bottle in his hand like a judge's gavel. "The story goes, he wanted nothing to do with those babies, so you moved back here and settled in, knowing that sooner or later he'd have to face them. And now you got what you wanted. He's forced to pretend to care, because there's no way Zeke and Belinda are going to let him abandon his own kids. Seems like you're in line for that big rodeo payday."

Rosie didn't actually implode at that, though it was close. She was pretty sure that she was *smoking* with rage.

"I don't need his money." There was smoke in her voice,

too. "You should know that already. I've been taking care of my babies just fine."

Jack only watched her, all of that cool, assessing steel, and it made her want to squirm around in her seat like a naughty little girl. It cost her something to keep from doing it.

She made herself shrug with an attempt at a nonchalance she certainly didn't feel. "I think that it's good for the boys to know him. I think it's good for him to have a relationship with them. He's their father, no matter what people think. The great news in all of this is that despite the shock of it all, everything with Ryder has been perfectly civilized."

At that, Jack let out a short, sharp laugh. "Has it now."

Rosie looked at him, frowning. "What does that mean?"

"Rosie." Her big brother looked at her with something a lot like pity in that gaze of his. "We're talking about a man who has spent the bulk of his adult life on the back of bucking bulls. For fun *and* profit."

"I don't have the slightest idea what you mean by that. I know what he does for a living." She shook her head. "How does that have anything to do with the situation?"

"Ryder Carey is not a civilized man," Jack told her, with a note of finality in his voice. "If you think he is, that can only mean one thing. He's just waiting for the right time to show you his real face."

That was the moment Matilda came charging in with the boys, and Rosie had to pretend that she hadn't felt a chill at

Jack's words, down deep into her soul. Making her feel brittle and cold, even when Jack stoked the fire.

But the following morning it was the boys' birthday, so there was no time to worry about Ryder's *true face*.

His actual face was problematic enough, and he presented it at the house later that day, with all of his family in tow.

One of the many civilized decisions that Ryder and Rosie had made was this one. Rather than overwhelm the boys with a stream of visitors coming by and being, in all likelihood, a little overly emotional in their presence, they decided to have this birthday party instead.

It had actually been Rosie's idea. Ryder had completely agreed.

The boys had taken cupcakes to their nursery school, and played with their little friends, like the famous Jacinta, but this evening party had a different agenda altogether.

It was still celebrating their birthday, but more than that, it was celebrating the fact that they were all family now.

Rosie bustled around, serving the cake on paper plates featuring Spider-Man, Eli's favorite, and Superman, Levi's hero.

"This is like the cocktail party from hell," Matilda muttered from beside her at one point as they hunched in the kitchen, maniacally putting together another tray of sweet treats.

Because obviously, any perilous emotional moment could be handled with enough sugar. Or at least a person could get through it that way.

"And how," Rosie muttered in reply.

Out in the living room, the boys were hopped up on cake and candy, and were loving holding court for all these new adults who hung on their every word.

Harlan had his arm around Kendall, who was looking a little misty eyed and a good bit rounder than the last time Rosie had seen her. But then, Zeke and Belinda were looking emotional too. They sat with Jack on the couch and made no bones about the fact that they were instantly and irrevocably in love with their grandchildren.

Rosie's cousins stood a line against the wall, like they thought this was an Old West saloon. On the other side of the room, she saw the younger Carey brothers, Boone and Knox, staring right back at them, like at any moment it might be time to draw a six-gun, or break out into fisticuffs.

"Ignore them," came a voice from beside her.

She glanced up and froze. She thought it was Ryder, but only for a second. Because this version was smiling. There was a particular gleam in his gaze that suggested a deep good humor, and she knew instantly that it was Wilder.

"I always do ignore them," she said. "As my longtime personal policy."

"Apparently," Wilder told her, as if they were buddies who always clustered together to talk like this, when they most certainly were not, "words were exchanged in the Copper Mine, feelings were hurt, panties were twisted, and now someone owes someone else an apology. Yet none are forthcoming."

"Sounds like every single night of the week of the Copper Mine," Rosie replied dryly.

"So it does," Wilder agreed. He crossed his arms, a smile on his face as he looked down at her. "Have to say, I really don't know how I missed it before, but it sure is something to see mirror images of my brother and me running around like this."

Rosie felt her smile shake a little. "I'm sorry."

"You don't have to be sorry," Wilder replied, and she could see that he meant it. "I know how my brother behaves."

What she wanted to say was that Wilder hadn't behaved all that differently himself, until recently. But he was a married man now. And Rosie had always thought that bringing up people's dirty pasts when they turned over a new leaf was mean. So she didn't say a word.

But there was suddenly another male body on her other side, and he was less careful.

"I can't help it if women find me fascinating," Ryder drawled at his twin. "I was never required to roll up on tourists and try to convince them that I was the cowboy of their dreams."

"You just had to make sure you were out of there before dawn," Wilder replied with a laugh. "If they saw you in the light, they might figure you out."

"Don't pay any attention to him," Ryder told Rosie. "He's always been jealous." He looked at Wilder again. "I can't help that I'm the pretty one."

Wilder only laughed at that, and as he did, Rosie let her shoulders creep back down from her ears. Because clearly, neither one of them was offended. In fact, if she looked closely, she was pretty sure that Ryder was even smiling.

"Got to get more cake," she muttered out loud, but when she turned around and rushed back into the kitchen, Ryder came with her.

"Are you good?" he asked her.

She didn't look over at him, not directly, but she was all too aware of him. He seemed to fill up the kitchen, as if his shoulders were so broad they were brushing against the walls. Even though she knew she was making that up in her head.

She knew it, so she turned around to face him, and that was worse.

Today he was wearing a long-sleeved T-shirt, jeans, and a fancy belt buckle that she didn't have to examine closely to know represented one of his many rodeo wins. Jack's words about his true face, and his lack of civilization, seemed to haunt her. It was like she was waiting for him to... shift. Become a wolf, right between the door to the living room and the kitchen table. Right here where he'd watched the kids eat meals and had started to see their less charming sides too, but still showed up every day.

He's a wolf, something in her repeated, a little too warmly. *And here you are, all dressed in red.*

The fairy tales wrote themselves.

And that was a line of thinking that could only lead to badness.

He was studying her, and as he did, his head tilted a little to one side.

Suddenly, everything between them changed.

Or maybe the truth was, they reverted back to their original factory settings.

Because this was the Ryder she'd met in Texas. This intoxicating drink of a man, packaged so exquisitely in jeans and a shirt just tight enough to remind her what it felt like to press her face against the hard wall of his chest.

This was the man she'd spent that whole, wondrous, life-altering night with. A night that she thought was tattooed into her skin and would be a part of her forever, and that was before she'd known she was pregnant.

But she was pretty sure that this wasn't Ryder showing her his true face. He hadn't been hiding it. This was her finally letting go of the blinders she'd been wearing since he'd showed up in the yard.

Because all she had been thinking about were the boys. What this would mean for them. How this would look like to everyone else. How she would tell her family. What she would do when his knew, too.

All of those things still swirled around her, even though the questions had largely been answered already, but now it was as if she could finally see the truth about herself again.

And the truth was this.

This taut, searing intensity that sparked between them, as if no time at all had passed between that night and now.

As if nothing could possibly matter as much as the sizzle of it. The crackle that worked its way down her limbs, blazed into her blood, and pooled with a white-hot intensity deep in her belly.

This was the truth. She had gone to that bull-riding expedition that night knowing that he would be there. Hoping that she would see him, because who wouldn't have a silly little crush on one of the Carey twins? She'd never met anyone who didn't.

And when she'd actually found herself standing in front of him, there had been this.

This glimmering, impossible thread between them that only pulled tighter and tighter all the time.

If it hadn't been for the boys, she would have noticed it sooner. Now that she did, she felt like she was wrapped up tight in the web of this. Like if she wasn't careful, she'd start shining so bright they'd be able to see her in space.

She could hear everyone else out in the living room. She could hear her boys shouting, and the mother in her was already calculating exactly how long they had left before the inevitable sugar crash.

But in the kitchen, where it was only the two of them, it was even louder. And neither one of them was saying a word.

"Keep looking at me like that," Ryder suggested in a low voice that connected, immediately and intensely, to all that bright heat. "And I think we both know exactly what's going to happen next."

Chapter Six

H E'D EXPECTED THAT stubborn chin of hers to come into play. He'd expected that she would frown at him in that way she did, that he'd noticed by now worked on the boys, too.

What he didn't expect was for her clear blue eyes to go… a little bit foggy. And then, as he stood there watching her intently, that same gaze dropped to his mouth.

And Ryder was not made of stone.

He had never pretended he was.

He moved toward her and then, anticipating an objection, he put his palm over the nape of her neck and guided her with him to the other side of the kitchen. Then, because it was March and bitterly cold outside, straight into the pantry.

"What… what are you doing?" she asked, but Ryder didn't answer her as he closed the door behind them.

Or rather, he did, but not with words.

He bent down, gathering that sleek body of hers against him, and took her mouth with his.

And one question was answered immediately.

Rosie was every bit as tempting as his memory had convinced him she was. She tasted like sugar and heat and he licked his way in, amazed to discover that he hadn't over exaggerated the power in this at all.

This had been the problem that night.

Kissing Rosie felt like coming home.

In Texas, he had assured himself that feeling was simply because she was literally from his hometown.

But this was Cowboy Point. And everything was different now. That feeling of homecoming seemed to wrap itself around him, then draw him in deeper.

Better still, she kissed him back.

And Ryder knew her better now. Certainly better than he had after one night of flirting, a couple of cocktails with a little bit of food, and then that wild rush of heat that had haunted him ever since.

That ghost of her that he'd never managed to escape.

Had he come here that day to apologize—or to see if she still haunted him years later?

Either way, he knew her better now than he had then. That meant he could marvel even more at how she kept herself so contained, so polished in her everyday life. That sleekness like a weapon.

But when his mouth was on her, she went wild.

Her kiss was ravenous. Their tongues tangled and she reached up to grab handfuls of his shirt, pulling him closer to her.

The fire between them was instant. The burst of need,

that blaze of longing, was close enough to overwhelming. It was a flame that seemed to reach higher and burn brighter than any he'd felt before—

There was a noise on the other side of the pantry door and Rosie jerked back, as if she'd suddenly been shocked by something electric.

"I swear I saw her come in here," came her sister Matilda's voice, perfectly audible through the door. "Maybe she went outside to get a little fresh air."

"The air isn't fresh, it's freezing cold," came another voice that Ryder recognized. Wyatt Stark.

"It's the poetry in your soul that makes you so compelling and not at all off-putting," Matilda replied. "Really."

And then she laughed at whatever the notably unpoetic Wyatt rumbled her way, in a low voice that didn't make it to the pantry door.

Inside, in the dark, Rosie tipped forward, pressing her forehead into Ryder's chest. She was still gripping his shirt, but now every muscle in her body was tense.

When there were no more sounds in the kitchen, she blew out a breath. She pushed back and touched her fingertips to her face, as if looking for cracks. Or evidence of that fire that had raged so high and hard between them.

"Rosie," he began.

She shushed him, but viciously. Her gaze snapped to his, and even in the dark of the pantry closet, he could see the expression she was shooting his way clearly. It was made of daggers, sharp and deadly.

"You will stay in this pantry," she told him, her voice brooking absolutely no argument and backed up with that frown that made him want to apologize without knowing what his infraction was. "You will count to one hundred. I will go out there, make sure the coast is clear, and hope that people think that you're the one that was outside in the snow, getting fresh air or dying of hypothermia."

"I'm known for that," he said, blandly. "Fresh, hypothermic March air is my favorite."

And he was shocked beyond measure—and something like delighted, if he was honest about it, when she hauled off and punched him.

Right in the gut. And hard.

Then winced, because there wasn't a lot of give in that area.

Rosie glared at him like he was the one slugging people. She shook her hand, and yanked it back when he went to take it in his.

"This is not a joke," she hissed at him. "Our very small children are in this house. And who are they with? Oh, that's right. Every single one of our family members. This is no time to be doing... *this*. In a *closet*."

"How exactly do you think that both of our families got so big?" he asked.

Innocently, he thought.

She looked like she wanted to punch him again, but

thought better of it.

"Count to one hundred, Ryder. Quietly."

Rosie moved around him and didn't look back as she eased open the door, glanced out, then swiped a packet of something unidentifiable from the shelf beside her as she walked back into the kitchen.

He leaned back against the door that she shut behind her with what felt like a little punch of temper. While he was at it, he flipped the lights on. And wasn't at all surprised to find that the pantry was as ruthlessly organized as everything else in this house.

Lines of cans, boxes neatly stacked. But he knew the truth that wasn't immediately clear from that sort of evidence. Rosie was a good cook. She liked her ingredients organized so she could toss them altogether and find a kind of art in the making of things.

Kind of like Rosie herself. She kept herself pretty much ruthlessly organized too. Yet he had the pleasure of knowing that just like any one of those boxes of spaghetti staring back at him, she was rigid and unbendable... until she heated up.

When he eased his way out of that pantry, having obediently counted to the prescribed one hundred, the kitchen was empty. He walked to the entryway that led into the living room and paused there, because everyone he cared about was there.

Everyone he cared about and the Starks, that was, though he grinned even as he thought it.

Eli and Levi were cuddled in between Belinda and Zeke on the couch. Ryder caught the old man's eye as he sat there, beaming down at his grandsons.

Zeke nodded. Ryder nodded back.

But inside, Ryder felt more than a little ashamed of the fact that he'd gone and yelled at his father in the workshop that night. He also understood that he was forgiven.

And for a moment, he got it.

This was the thing his father had always wanted. This feeling inside of him, that sat on him so heavily but didn't feel smothering, was love.

He'd felt it immediately when he'd understood who the twins were. He felt it now, looking at his sons chattering earnestly to their grandfather, his father.

Ryder felt *connected* when that was a word, a feeling, he had really only ever associated with his twin. This connection was different. Bigger. It was a link to the world, and to his family, and to the march of humanity across the planet in ways that he'd heard people talk about before, but had always thought sounded made up.

He got it now.

And over in the corner, talking intently with Cat and Kendall, stood the reason why.

Rosie.

Rosie, who'd made this happen. And though he might have wished that it had happened in a way that hadn't left her on her own with two babies, thinking that was how it was going to be for her forever, he couldn't be sorry that it happened at all. How could he?

She looked up from her conversation and he didn't understand how he could be the only man in this room who seemed to see that particular sparkle in her eyes. Surely everyone here could tell, just from looking at how her flushed cheeks were, that she'd had his tongue in her mouth not long before.

His phone buzzed in his pocket, and he pulled it out, not at all surprised to find that it was a text from Wilder though he sat across the room, seemingly paying attention to whatever it was Jack Stark and Harlan were talking about.

Weird how you and your baby mama disappeared from the party at the same time. I'm sure that's coincidental.

Maybe one day when you have children, Ryder texted back, *assuming you ever reach that level of maturity, you'll understand why it is that sometimes, the grown-ups have to have a private talk.*

He and Wilder texted like this all the time. Wherever they went, whatever they did. It was part of the lifelong conversation they'd always been in, and always would be in.

But it was particularly entertaining tonight, when he could stand across the room and watch his brother laugh when he read what Ryder had sent him.

I'm sure that's it, Wilder texted back. *I'm sure that's not euphemistic at all.*

That's an awfully big word, Ryder replied. *I'm the pretty one, remember?*

And he had to consider the evening a win.

The routine he'd fallen into, here in this new phase of his life, took on a different shape after the boys' party. He got up most mornings and tagged along with one or other of his brothers, getting a feel for the ranch again. Midmorning, he headed to Rosie's, where the twins called him *Daddy* in their excited, high-pitched voice, and solicited his opinion on everything of importance to them that day, from their other brother's perfidy, to the clothes they wanted to wear, to things the infamous Jacinta had said a nursery school. There were usually reports of any silly things their mother might have done.

One morning she looked frazzled when he got there, unusual for the polished Rosie Stark, so he got the boys ready for their nursery school himself. He led them out the door to her car, which he used to drive them down into Cowboy Point because she was the one who had the car seats. He was going to have to upgrade his truck.

After he dropped them off, with a bland smile at the raised eyebrows of the nursery school teacher who met the boys at the door, he decided the car itself was a disaster. And he had some concerns about how it was running, so he drove it down to Marietta, sweet talked his way into a mechanic's shop since he happened to know the guy in charge from back in high school, and washed and cleaned it out himself.

When he came back to Rosie's house, she was less frazzled, but more irritated.

"Where have you been?" she demanded, standing there in her front doorway, letting all her heat out into the cold, gloomy day.

"Your car was a disaster," he told her. "I fixed it."

"What do you mean, you fixed it?"

He sauntered toward her, aware on some level that he really shouldn't find these moments of domesticity so much damned fun, but he did. "You know, I really question each and every one of your cousins, not to mention your brother, that they've been letting you drive around in that thing."

"*That thing* is an incredibly dependable vehicle that has stood the test of time," she shot back, hotly. Like he'd insulted her honor, her family, and her first born.

"Well, now it will stand it even better," he drawled as he reached her at the door. "You're welcome."

And she was scowling at him, but she was so cute with her hair pulled back and that confection of a pink sweater that she was wearing today. Not to mention a pair of jeans that never failed to do a number on him, so he really had no choice at all but to pull her into his arms and kiss her until she forgot that she was mad at him.

Sometimes he came back in the afternoon when she was done with her job, so he could see the boys when they got home and hang around for dinner, too. Other times he went home and had dinner at the ranch, with whatever configuration of family was around of an evening. Still other times he spent time with Wilder and Cat, playing the card games they seemed to love so much.

"Dangerous prospect, playing cards with a Lisle," he said to Wilder. Pretty much every time.

"He likes it when I cheat," Cat said with a wink. "He thinks it's hot."

"Ryder doesn't have an opinion on your hotness," Wilder told her, shaking his head, though his mouth twitched. "Do you?"

He didn't even have to look at Ryder as he asked it. Ryder kept his gaze on his cards. "What's hot?" he asked. "Anyway, I'm blind."

"As a bat," Wilder told his wife. Then he threw his cards on the table. "And also, enjoy this royal flush."

Ryder liked each of these different sorts of evenings in their own ways, and far more than he would have believed he could if he'd tried to tell any past version of him that this was his future. He'd always maintained that what he loved was the road, but it turned out that letting himself settle into what he already had felt even better than another new, temporary city and nothing to think about but bull riding and, if he didn't break anything, a little companionship on the other side.

It was funny how little appeal that kind of night held now. Usually he felt restless after a weekend anywhere, and yet here he was over a month back home and he didn't have even the faintest hint of that usual itch.

And of all the evenings he got to have here, the ones he

loved the most involved him lying in a narrow little twin bed in the boys' room, with each of them pressed up tight beside him as he read them one book, then another.

He loved the ease of their affection, uncomplicated and trusting, pressing into him like they were a part of him in ways that transcended biology.

Another thing that would have panicked him to contemplate a year ago—hell, even two months ago—and these days, made him feel something perilously close to the happiest he'd ever been.

Because he liked to read them stories, and he liked the way they listened so intently, and corrected him as he went. But what he really liked was to look up toward the doorway to find Rosie standing there with her heart in her eyes once more.

Every time he did, it shifted things inside him.

The more time he spent with his new little family, the more he questioned himself about the ways that he'd operated in his own family all his life. Because this instant family deal of his was great. He loved these kids. They fascinated him and entertained him. They were their own little people, and it was something like awe-inspiring to see the way they learned their way in such a big world all around them. He and Rosie would put the boys to sleep, then he would follow her downstairs. And then, if Matilda wasn't around, the two of them would end up stretched out on that couch in her living room, driving each other crazy.

Rosie insisted they stay dressed. Ryder, happily, had always been a creative thinker.

Every night it seemed to get hotter, better, in a way that really should have alarmed him.

But it didn't.

It was like he'd been waiting for this his whole life.

One typically frigid morning, he and Wilder sat in Wilder's truck, bumping around through snowy pastures. until Ryder found himself something like emotional as he gazed out at the splendor of this place. Snowcapped mountains in every direction. The sweep of this land that had been in his family's hands for generations.

It all felt like it landed in him differently, now. He could imagine taking his own boys on a tour like this, making sure that they knew that they were connected to the sky so big, the mountains so tall and watchful, and the sheer courage and grit it took to carve out a life in between the two.

"You must be clawing at the walls," Wilder said. When Ryder only lifted a brow, his twin laughed. "Last time you stayed in Cowboy Point this long, you had a calendar on the bedroom wall where you marked off each day like you were in prison."

At first Ryder had no idea what he was talking about. Then he laughed, too. "I was a teenager."

"It's not like you stuck around when you weren't a teenager any longer, though, is it?"

There was no heat in that question, no guilt trip or underlying attempt to shame Ryder one way or the other. Maybe that was why it resonated the way it did.

"Things are different now," Ryder said after a moment or two. "There's Dad, first and foremost. That's why I came back."

Wilder only shook his head at that, his mouth flattening out. "I still find it hard to believe."

Ryder couldn't go there. "I don't want to believe it. Maybe I think the longer I stay here, the longer he'll live, because he's always complaining I only come home for the big things. Weddings. Funerals."

They both laughed, sort of. Funerals weren't very funny anymore.

The truck slid over an icy patch, and Wilder let it, then had them bumping along again when the patch of ice let them go.

"Do you know you're going to do?" he asked.

Ryder was fully aware that this was the same sort of question that his brothers had all been waiting to ask him that day that he'd done an end run around their little intervention. He'd had to deal with each and every one of them individually after that, but he thought he'd gotten the better end of the deal by not having them come at him in a pack.

Individually, they'd all pretty much said the same thing. Harlan had expressed surprise, but also concern, for both Ryder and Rosie. Wilder had been outraged that Ryder had never told him that he'd seen Rosie down in Austin. He wanted to know what else Ryder had kept from him, *desecrating the twin bond*, as he put it. And he hadn't liked it much when Ryder had rolled his eyes.

So Ryder had rolled them even more.

Boone had been gruffly concerned about the rumors he'd heard in town, all of which, he was quick to tell Ryder, he'd been certain to correct. *Because I know you're no deadbeat dad*, Boone had said with that quiet intensity of his. *And now they know it too.*

It was Knox who had looked at him curiously, and then asked, *Do you* want *to be a father?*

Like it was a choice.

But the unspoken part of all of his conversations was the inevitable truth that Ryder would leave again. That this was a break he was taking to look after Zeke. Or at least to be around while Zeke was declining, because it wasn't like the old man let anyone take care of him in any real sense.

The Ryder they all knew had never resisted the call of the road. None of his brothers even thought to question the possibility that he might be done with it.

In point of fact, he hadn't actually thought that himself, until this moment.

Until his twin asked him what he was going to do, out here where the sky was too big and the mountains too tall and every breath felt like eternity.

"I could do another tour," Ryder said, feeling it out as he said it. "But I'm already the old man in the mix. Every ride I take increases my chance of serious injury and the older I get, the less likely I am to recover well."

"You're telling me things I already know," Wilder replied, lazily. "What I don't know is how you lasted this long."

"Spite," Ryder drawled, but he smiled as he said it. "Sheer stubbornness."

His twin laughed, but there was something darker in his gaze. "Because coming back home would be a fate worse than death, got it."

Ryder thought about that a lot later that night. He had dinner with his father, alone, because Belinda had gone out to one of her club meetings. Garden club, book club, wine club, it was hard to say. Belinda was a woman of many passions.

Zeke and he talked about sports, the weather, the ranch.

They did not discuss health. They didn't even stray close to the topic. Maybe a better son would have pushed, Ryder thought—but he only knew how to be the son he was.

After they ate, they cleared away their dishes and neatened up the kitchen because it was that or face Belinda's wrath—and no one wanted to deal with Belinda's wrath, or even the faintest hint of her annoyance. She was not the sort of woman who kept her feelings inside. Standing there in the sparkling, clean kitchen, Ryder thought to ask his father a question that never would have occurred to him to ask before.

"I can't remember why I was so determined to leave this town when I did," he said, looking at one of the pictures of him and Wilder on the wall. He had no idea which one of them was which, since they had dressed as twin cowboys for Halloween that year. "Can you?"

Zeke smiled, though there was something sad about it. "Your mother died here. Don't you remember?"

"That she died?" Ryder shook his head. "Yeah, Dad. I remember that."

"When she died, you and your brother got it in your head—"

He shook that off, but Ryder knew what he meant—or he thought he did, anyway. He didn't think he or Wilder had ever talked about it with anyone else, but the fact was, they'd been six years old and hard to handle at the best of times, and they had likely caused their mother more stress in her final days than she needed.

There was no point talking about it, that was just the way it had been.

The way Zeke looked at him now made something in him think good and hard about shivering, though he fought it off. "You told me once, around that time, that this was a bad place. When I asked you why, you said it was because it took her."

Ryder felt that land. So hard and so intense it was as if Zeke had picked up a crowbar and plunged it straight through his ribs.

The worst part was that his father's gaze on his was kind. And knowing in the way Wilder's had been, too, like the only mystery here was the stuff Ryder insisted on not letting himself see. About himself.

"I always thought," Zeke told him quietly, "that you figured if you ran around hard enough, fast enough, and long enough, you'd find a way to outrun death."

Ryder thought he would prefer it if his father had picked up one of the cast-iron pans and whacked him in the face with it.

He made it out of the ranch house and into his truck, but truth be told, he wasn't sure he really paid any attention to what he was doing until he was off Carey land and making his way up that hill toward the lodge.

On the other side, he didn't think. There was no one else on the road so he pulled out his cell phone and texted Rosie.

When he got to her house, she came outside to meet him with a heavy coat wrapped around her but not zipped up. She peered in his window, frowning.

"What's going on?" she asked. "Why did you want me to come out here?"

"Are the kids okay? Is your sister home?"

Rosie's frown deepened. "Yes and yes, but—"

"Get in."

He belted out the order and he watched her blink, take it in, consider telling him what he could do with his order— and then decide to obey him anyway.

And it was a fine thing, it turned out, to know a woman well enough to see the things she *didn't* do right there on his face.

It felt like another intimacy he hadn't known enough to understand he was missing, because it had never occurred to him that friendship and family could go along with heat and sex and longing. He had seen those smug expressions on other men's faces and he'd thought they were nuts. *Poor fools*, he'd thought, to get themselves locked down like that when there was a whole world out there.

He hadn't gotten it.

He never would have gotten it, but now there was Rosie.

And there were so many worlds in this one woman.

Too many worlds.

A man could spend a lifetime and not explore the half of them.

She walked around his truck, climbed in, and sat there in silence as he pulled back out of the driveway. He didn't head back toward the lodge, but took the road that wound its way in and around the trees that dotted the mountainside. He kept going until he found an old lookout he vaguely remembered from high school.

He pulled in, turned his truck's lights off but kept the engine running, and then he turned to her.

"Ryder. Are you okay? What is happening?"

"There are rules in your house," he said, his voice low. He unbuckled himself from his seat belt and reached over to unbuckle hers. "I'm sick of the rules, Rosie."

Then he pulled her across the bench seat, dragged her over his lap, and got his mouth on her, where it belonged. While he was at it, he got his hands beneath that coat and the turtleneck she wore beneath it.

And he decided that if he was going to experiment with all these worlds, and all that intensity, for as long as he was home—he'd be doing it like this.

Chapter Seven

ROSIE KNEW THAT she really should stop this. That would be the wise decision.

But wisdom when it came to Ryder had gone out the window a long time ago. Back in Austin years ago, if she was going to be brutally honest about it.

And over these past few weeks, ever since they'd kissed like they were already naked in her pantry, of all places, well.

She'd felt as if she was slowly burning alive.

More alarming, she couldn't say that she regretted a single moment of it. And now it was as if he'd reached into the depths of her mind, rummaged around in the dreams that had been haunting her for years, and found one of her favorites.

The two of them, wrapped around each other like this.

In the front seat of his truck, like a country song.

Rosie figured a girl never really knew who she was until a beautiful man had her pressed up hard against him in the dark cab of a pickup truck with the heat on and nothing else to do but surrender herself into his hands.

He had been surprisingly, deliciously talented at getting his hands in all kinds of places on the couch, while never *quite* breaking the rules she'd made. She should have found that to be evidence of his boundary pushing and inability to listen, but instead, she found she admired him for maintaining the letter of the law while making them both a little bit too giddy.

When she would have sworn up and down—and had—that she would never let herself get silly over a man again.

But this was Ryder.

And in her house, she was always still the mother. *Mommy.* At any moment, she could expect to hear one of the kids crying, so everything always felt rushed. Furtive. Like she was getting away with something and would likely pay for it—

She knew instantly that this was something different.

"Don't you have a house somewhere?" she asked, smiling a little bit ruefully against his mouth.

"I do," he said, still close. As if he couldn't bear to move away any more than she could. "I have an Airstream and it's too far away."

Then he kissed her again, taking it even more slowly. Making it impossible to kiss him back with the same depth and greed and excitement that she could feel all over her, like some kind of delicious fever.

He moved his mouth from hers, finding a trail down her neck, and then, muttering something beneath his breath that sounded marvelously impatient—a move in the right direction, to her mind—he stripped off her coat and tossed it aside. Then the practical turtleneck she was wearing, though he did seem to take a moment of reverence as he traced the shape of it down the length of her body. But he peeled it off and tossed it aside, and then, his dark eyes rising to meet hers, he took off her bra, too.

It was only then that it occurred to her that her body was different now. Changed since the last time he'd seen it.

But any momentary twinge of something like embarrassment that she might have been tempted to feel was gone in an instant, because he made a noise that was all longing and delight, and she was surprised she didn't come apart at the sound.

Maybe she nearly did.

He bent his head, used his hands to lift her breasts to his mouth, and then he feasted.

Rosie had nothing to do. Nowhere to go, no children to handle.

No one was going to interrupt them up here in the woods, where the local sheriff's deputy only bothered to patrol in better weather, looking for errant teens.

There was nothing on earth to do but enjoy this man that she'd been aching for since the last time she'd seen him, in too many different ways to count—

But especially in this way, because this was even better than she remembered.

And maybe, just maybe, she could forgive herself for throwing her whole life off course, because here she was, in full possession of the knowledge of what came from this behavior, more than ready to do it again.

Rosie was straddling him on the bench seat of his truck, there was no lying to herself anymore, and all she needed to do was surrender to him.

So she did.

She arched back, throwing her hands back to brace herself on the dash. That had the glorious effect of giving him more of what he wanted while there between her legs, it allowed her to press into that hard, glorious ridge of his.

And, at last, not worry about someone walking in on them.

She didn't know when she began to rock herself against him, or maybe she'd been doing it all along.

It felt so good, and not enough. She felt as if her body was impatient all on its own. It knew where this was headed and it wanted him so badly that it didn't care what she was doing.

She was fully on board.

Body. Mind.

Maybe her soul too, now that she considered it.

His mouth was a magical torture. Rosie hardly recognized the sound she was making as he played with her and teased her. Taunted her, over and over, then brought his teeth into the mix just to make it a little more spicy. Just a scrape.

Just enough to make her writhe against him, her voice rough like a stranger's.

She could feel him grow bigger and thicker against her. Even harder than before, when surely that should have been impossible.

Rosie rocked and she rocked. She felt his hands move to the front of her jeans, felt her waistband give a little with a single expert tug, and then one of his hands was sliding down the back to grab hold of her bottom to take that rocking motion to a whole new level.

It had been so long.

And he seemed to know what she needed so well.

Because she shattered, just like that. She shook against him and lost herself in the roll and tumble, dropping her head forward so her face was near his.

He kissed her and kissed her, and then everything became something of a scramble as they awkwardly stripped off clothes with hands that were a little too excited for the task. As they bumped into each other, and laughed, and paused to kiss each other hungrily, deeply.

Ryder pushed back one of the seats to lay flat, and then picked her up and moved her into the backseat as if she weighed about as much as that turtleneck that he'd tossed aside before, like a feather.

He followed, and he was a big man, but he found a way to fit them both there. It was closer. It was awkward and it was perfect and then, finally, he was on top of her once more. Rosie could wrap her legs around him, and feel the press of his hard body, his golden skin, and that beautiful, impossibly hard chest of his as he lay over her.

But all he did was stay there, hold her face in his hands, and kiss her.

Tenderly. Sweetly.

It made her want to cry.

More, it reminded her how it had been that night, when he had done something a lot like this. It had been a wild, bright burst of passion and chemistry. And then, later, they'd gotten out of the shower and he'd taken it upon himself to seat her before him, still naked, while he brushed out her hair.

Then he'd turned her, so gently, and kissed her just like this.

Rosie had taken whole years to accept the fact that it was that very moment that made her believe, so foolishly, that she'd fallen in love with him.

She was a lot older now, far older than mere years could attest, and infinitely more wise—whether she wanted to be or not. She wasn't the same girl she'd been then, made entirely of wishes and hopes, expectations and pie-in-the-sky dreams.

This version of Rosie had two boys to raise in this world, and she'd thought all along that she'd be doing that alone. This Rosie had stopped dreaming and had gotten tough. This Rosie was certain that she could weather any storm, because she already had.

But this wasn't a storm.

This was a tender fall of a lovely rain. It washed all over her, sweet like summer. It swept its way deep inside her, flooding her, until she thought she could feel all of those padlocks she'd put on her heart let go all at once.

As if, all this time, they'd been worried about keeping out intruders and villains and *him*, but he found her anyway.

One raindrop at a time.

One sweet kiss after the next.

He lifted his head. His eyes were glittering, dark and glorious. Rosie couldn't bring herself to look away.

She thought about what she'd imagined he'd be like, once he found out the truth. All those scenarios she'd played out in her head during all of those night feedings, all of those too-early mornings.

Instead, he'd fallen in love with the boys in one fell swoop.

She'd watched it happen.

Rosie had tried to have boundaries. She'd tried to keep things civilized. She'd tried so hard.

But now she watched as he reached into the front seat of the truck and pulled protection out of the back pocket of the jeans he'd tossed aside. She watched as he rolled it on over him, winced a little, and settled himself between her legs once more.

"I want to make sure—" he began.

"I swear to God," Rosie gritted out at him. "If you don't—"

And she shattered all over again, into even tinier pieces than before, when he pushed his way inside.

It took a long time to come back to herself. When she did, he laughed and pulled her in closer to him so he could wrap her up, get his mouth on hers, and only then begin to move.

And this time, he didn't take it slow.

This time, he pounded into her hard and wild, so she could do nothing but wrap her legs around him, lock her ankles tight, and enjoy the ride.

He threw her from the peak of one flame straight into another, and it was a rush, a magic and dizzying gallop—

And the next time she broke apart, he came with her.

She heard her name in his mouth as they both spun out, yet still clung to each other. She thought maybe she shouted his.

Anything was possible and everything was blurry. Rosie was limp. When she finally came back to herself, they were sitting there in the back of his truck. Ryder had somehow managed to pull on his jeans and wrap her in his flannel shirt, and now he held her on his lap.

She rested her head against his shoulder and listened to his heart beat beneath her ear.

Her hair had fallen down from its usual ruthless ponytail and he was running his fingers through it, playing with the strands.

Rosie's heart was so full she was surprised it didn't spill

right out of her.

And she thought, *this has been a terrible mistake.*

But she accepted that. With one of her hands, she traced the shape of his nearest pectoral muscle, then followed it down lower so she could move her fingers over the impressive ridges in his hard, strong abdomen.

The trouble was, she had been bad at not falling in love with him that one night. Really bad at it, in fact.

And now she was in a situation that was much, much worse.

Because this was pretty much all the things she had pretended—for years—that she never wanted. She had forced herself to believe that she was better off without him, and she *had* believed it. She had made sure she believed it… during the light of day.

At night, always, different temptations raised their heads and made her wonder if she was just kidding herself—

But no. It was exactly this that she'd convinced herself she didn't want, because she'd known she couldn't have it.

Ryder here, back home in Cowboy Point. Ryder engaged with Eli and Levi, being a father, loving them. Loving them so much that sometimes she forgot that she and he *weren't* together as they sat reading them stories at night, or eating dinners together.

She had pretended, ferociously, that she was perfectly fine without all this.

But that was a lie.

And it was a lie that she'd continued to cling to, before that kiss.

Though now she'd gone and ruined everything. Because what she prided herself on most of all was being *practical*.

It didn't matter that there was kissing, or adventures with clothes on out there on the living room couch, because it was just a bit of silliness at the end of an evening. It didn't mean anything. That was what she'd been telling herself.

As long as she kept it all practical, with their focus firmly on the boys, then what did it matter?

It's fine as long as you don't have sex with him, she had lectured herself every night when he'd left, standing there with her back pressed against the door until she heard his truck pull away. *All this is and ever can be is a little bit of fun. And you deserve it.*

The very last thing she needed to do was the things she'd just done, and so heedlessly. So recklessly. So *deliberately*.

Not because it wasn't good, because if it could be any better it would likely kill her. But because it turned out that she couldn't handle herself when it came to this man.

She had fallen in love with him that night in Austin. She had hated him for a lot of years in between.

And now…

Well, she told herself primly. *It was just one mistake. It doesn't even count.*

But when she lifted her head, Ryder was gazing down at her with that familiar, too-hot glint in his dark gaze.

Rosie knew she should stop this, immediately.

Surely she *meant* to.

But instead, when he shifted her around on his lap, she offered no word of protest when he rolled protection over himself once more. Not only did she not protest, she was the one who shifted herself up on her knees and reached down between them, so she could fit him right where she wanted him.

Just like she was the one who sank down on him, immediately, and then groaned the same way he did.

With relief and delight, as if it had been years instead of less than an hour.

She knew better, she really did.

But Rosie was the one who began to move, and she was the one who set the pace, and when he told her to slow down she laughed and went faster.

Until he clamped his hands around her hips, and made her wait.

And when they finally found that white-hot finish once again, she told herself that it was *fine*, because it was only one night.

Just one night, out in his truck, where it didn't even count.

And that was what she continued to tell herself, just about every night thereafter. Every chance they got.

As it turned out, they got a lot of chances. Or maybe they made their own chances, it was hard to tell.

Rosie assured herself that she could stop any time. She was positive that she could. She told herself so, over and over again, every time they set themselves on fire.

As if one of these nights, it would finally be true.

Chapter Eight

MARCH BLUSTERED ALONG, though Ryder barely felt the cold. Like everyone else, he got a little too excited when there were a couple of nice days or even a lovely afternoon, but this was Montana. Winter always came back, and it usually came back hard.

One day, after Wilder and Ryder made a run down into Marietta for some supplies, they stopped at Mountain Mama Pizza on the way back. The last time Ryder had been in town, the rambling yet cozy pizza place had still been trying to hold on to the fleeting promise of good fall weather. They had still had their patio open with strands of lights strung all around and the doors wide open to welcome in the outside.

But it was March now, and fully winter no matter how close the so-called official first day of spring was. All the outside parts of the restaurant were closed up tight, leaving only the warm, bright interior that felt comfortable rather than crowded, even when it was full.

There were no free tables and only a few extra chairs at one. But as that one happened to be where the three Stark brothers sat, Ryder was already figuring that they'd get their food to go.

Wilder, naturally, had other ideas. He went, grabbed a seat, and plopped himself right down amongst the Starks as if he couldn't see the looks on their faces.

"Gentlemen," he drawled. "Maybe you haven't heard, but I single-handedly ended the feud between the Careys and the Lisles. I'm not in the mood to pick up another one. Get over it."

Ryder took the seat next to him, smiling blandly at Rosie's cousins.

For a moment, they all sat there, like they were waiting to see if their genetic links to old West varmints and vagabonds might take them over... but no. They were Montanans, sure, and that could mean a hardheaded feud.

Today it trended more toward a grizzled practicality that came of long winters that could take anyone out in a moment of indecision. Better to keep your affairs in order and your enemies so close they really were friends.

Or something like that.

"The thing about Rosie is that she was supposed to do huge things," Logan said, breaking into the silence at their table, though Fleetwood Mac was encouraging everyone to go their own damn way from the speakers.

"I'm sorry that you don't find my children to be enough of an achievement," Ryder replied, blandly enough.

Logan muttered something under his breath. "That's not what I meant."

"Tennessee and Dallas Lisle were not exactly overjoyed

when they discovered that I was dating their sister," Wilder said, almost offhandedly, though there was nothing *offhand* about the way he looked from one Stark brother to the next. "I thought there might come a time they wanted to punch me in the face. But they didn't."

"You boys can try to punch me in the face," Ryder offered. "That might be entertaining."

"I would like to know your intentions," Noah said formally, looking at Ryder intently. "I would like you to tell us all, right now, what your intentions are toward Rosie and those boys."

"Our boys," Logan said.

"Stark boys," Wyatt added, clearly just to be provocative.

Ryder decided not to give him what he wanted. He didn't rise to the bait, little as he liked his sons being called by a name that wasn't his—not that this was the time to worry about that little detail. "My intentions are none of your business," he said, but without any heat. "Given that this is a family situation, here's what I'll tell you. Those are my sons. I intend to be in their life for as long as I draw breath. That's what you need to know."

The three brothers glanced at each other, and looked like they were about to start talking again.

Ryder got there first. "Whatever happens between me and Rosie, or doesn't, is our business. Though I appreciate you all looking out for her. I'm not sure why you let her drive around in that death trap of a hatchback for so long when she needed new brakes, but still. I'm glad somebody is looking out for her in some capacity."

As intended, that started up a hot debate amongst the Starks about who had failed Rosie in regard to her vehicle. When his phone buzzed, he knew who it was. He looked down and Wilder's text was on his screen. *Nicely played.*

He nodded at his brother, but kept his eyes on Stark brothers.

After they ate, and some form of peace accord had been brokered—enough that everyone was talking about grabbing a drink at the Copper Mine at some point to celebrate the end of the hostilities—Wilder wanted to head down the snowy street to the new medical clinic, where Cat was managing the office for the new doctor in town, Ramona Taylor.

"Who I'm pretty sure is dating Knox," Wilder said as the two of them stood outside in the bitter cold, stamping their feet to encourage them to warm up. "Or was. He definitely was at some point last fall."

"I thought you said she was a doctor," Ryder said. When Wilder nodded, he grinned. "I thought doctors were smart."

Wilder laughed. "You haven't seen this doctor. Knox is an idiot to let her get away."

Ryder nodded. "Knox is an idiot, yes."

When Wilder headed down toward the clinic that was in a renovated old house that had belonged to a man he'd once thought was the local boogey man, he crossed over toward the general store. Now that he wasn't rushing to leave, he found that spending time in Cowboy Point made him feel good.

Ryder didn't know why, but suddenly, nostalgia didn't make him feel restless.

He liked seeing the Copper Mine, where he'd spent more than a few misspent nights on his rare visits home, tucked back on the other side of the creek. The creek was frozen now, and if Ryder remembered it correctly, that added a whole other level to the typical foolishness that went on there. He'd slid down it a time or two himself, in a less-than-coherent state.

Then there was the general store itself, the supposedly purloined building that had been the source of strife between his family and the Lisles for ages. He could see lights on in the diner next to the store, where, rumor was, Tennessee Lisle served up a mean breakfast and a good lunch when he was in the mood. Not that Ryder would know, having historically never darked the door of a Lisle establishment unless forced to use the store in a snowstorm or some such event. If he looked up, he could see that ridiculous lighthouse up on the top of Lisle Hill.

Today it made him smile.

He ducked into the feed store, thinking that he could find something fun to give the boys to play with, and found himself abruptly face-to-face with a woman he had the immediate feeling that he ought to recognize. Though he didn't.

"Ryder," she said in an ingratiating tone.

She reached out and put her hand on his arm, which he found he didn't like at all. He moved away, but kept a smile on his face, because there was no reason not to be polite in a small town. It always came back at you.

The woman searched his face, and then laughed. "It's me. Gwen Sheen. You remember me. I was *this close* to asking you to go to the Sadie Hawkins dance that year."

Ryder did not remember Gwen. Not the way she meant. She had rounded eyes that protruded slightly, a lot of wavy brown hair, and was only because of the older woman back behind the counter that he realized that he certainly knew her mother. And that he recognized the name.

Of course, this being the tiny town that it was, recognizing a name and being on nodding acquaintance with the person's mother meant that he knew everything there was to know about Gwen whether he remembered her or not. If she'd been anywhere near to asking him to anything, he'd never had a clue. Still, other details about her dropped into place anyway, like the words to a song he hadn't sung in ages.

He knew that she was younger than him and Wilder and he had a strong feeling she was somewhere between Boone and Knox. She was Marla Sheen's daughter, which meant that when good old Bear Sheen, the town drunk, drank too much to take himself indoors that one winter, Gwen had lost her father. He could tell from a glance that she'd never left

Cowboy Point and had no intention to. That wasn't a value judgment—it was more like a filing system. Things a person could know about another, just like that.

When she moved forward once again, and replaced her hand on his arm, he knew more.

"I just want to tell you that I've been thinking about you," she said, lowering her voice. "Everyone feels *so badly* for you, Ryder."

He had no idea what she was talking about. He moved his arm again, and didn't smile quite so much. "I sure appreciate that, Gwen. But I'm fine. More than fine, really. Thanks, though."

"It's okay," she said, and did something with her face that made him think that if he had been even slightly smaller, she would have attempted to pat him on the head, or something equally inappropriate. "You don't have to pretend. I'm an old friend. It's just *really, really* impressive, and *so* honorable that even though she trapped you, you're making the best of it. Honestly, you're an inspiration."

"It was a pleasure to see you, Gwen," Ryder lied.

He walked away from her, shaking his head, and decided the boys were fine without something from the feed store.

Later that evening, he and Rosie sat in the living room while Matilda wafted around the house, picking up and dropping the threads of the stories she was telling them the same way she did with the layers of her outdoor clothing.

She was banging around in the kitchen now, throwing

together a late dinner for herself. Rosie had just recently stopped insisting that they needed to keep a stern distance between them, and was sitting next to him on the couch.

Not exactly cuddling, but touching.

These were the kind of baby steps he liked.

Matilda liked to watch anything featuring animals, so that was on the television while Rosie read her books. Every time he came over, she was into a new one. He didn't think he'd ever met anyone in his life who read as fast or with as much delight as she did.

Earlier, after he'd gotten back to the ranch with Wilder, unloaded their supplies, and checked in on his father, he had gone back down to Rosie's. She'd told him that the boys were going straight from nursery school to the library with her cousin Sara Jane, who was holding the monthly read-along for the little kids.

When he got to her house, she was just getting out of the shower, preparing to go and catch the end of story hour.

They're with your cousin, he said. *You can be a little late.*

He'd picked her up, so hot and damp from the shower, and carried her into her bedroom. Then he'd spread her out on her queen-sized bed and followed her down onto the mattress.

After all the times in the truck, or quick and dirty moments in the bathroom with the lock thrown, it felt like an upgrade.

It was like paradise to have all of her like that. He exulted in it. It was possible he lost his mind a little, in the joy and endless magic that was Rosie.

You made me very late, she told him when she got out of the shower a second time, but she was smiling. And she'd run out the door, yelling over her shoulder that he should stay for dinner.

While she was gone, he'd changed the sheets and made her bed. Then he'd gone down to the living room, and picked up the paperback with the cracked spine lying there on the coffee table. He'd started reading the first chapter and it wasn't until the boys came running in, shouting *Daddy, Daddy*, because they'd seen his truck in the drive, that he realized that he was entirely content.

So far from *trapped* that he hardly knew what the word meant.

But now, after the usual rounds of dinner and baths and books, he worried that Rosie was maybe not so content.

After all, she'd had to do this on her own. He'd had her here for the beginning of his participation in their children's lives, guiding him along the way. So when Matilda looked at her phone—bolting up and knocking her bowl of popcorn onto the floor—then announcing she had to go save a cat, Ryder took it as an opportunity.

"Do you feel trapped?" he asked.

Rosie froze. She had been walking back into the living room after dispensing with Matilda's popcorn, and she stopped as surely as if he'd plunked a wall down in front of her. "What are you talking about?"

"I'm talking about this. Us."

"You're going to have to be more specific," Rosie said, carefully.

He leaned back against the couch and regarded her closely. "You came home that summer from college. Everything changed. Do you resent that?"

"I love those boys more than I ever thought it was possible to love anything," she told him immediately, low and intent.

"That's not what I asked you."

She looked away, then back at him as if she wasn't sure what to make of him, or this. She loosened up enough to come closer and sit down on the couch, curling her legs beneath her.

Still looking at him, she started to say something, then stopped.

But he didn't jump in.

He let her think it through, and eventually, she let out a small sound, like a sigh. "I know what you're asking, but I'm not that girl anymore. Do I mourn her sometimes? I guess. But everyone has to grow up sometime. Maybe it doesn't look the way I imagined it would, but what life does? Any time I try to take a tally, my blessings outweigh my challenges." She nodded, as if putting some punctuation on that statement. "I have to take that as a win. I do."

"Are there dreams you wish you could have pursued?"

"Of course there are," she said with a laugh. "Doesn't everybody have dreams they've outgrown? I love dancing. Watching it, I mean. I like to think that if only this was different or that was different, I could have been a phenomenal dancer, but I doubt it, because I never practiced. And every time I've been forced to dance against my will, I'm pretty sure I'm entirely made of left feet. So sure. That's a dream I'll never realize in this lifetime."

"One of your cousins told me today that you were going places. I guess I'm just sorry that it's my fault you ended up back here."

"Ryder. I like it here." Her eyes moved all over him, and it felt like some kind of caress, even though she was sitting on the next sofa cushion over. "I've always liked it here. I think that I've built the boys and me a pretty good life. It's sustainable. It's dependent on me, so if this never happened—" she gestured awkwardly between them, and he found that charming "—they'd be good. I'd be good."

"So what do you dream about now?"

It wasn't just a casual question. Maybe he was a little more attached to her answer than he meant to be, because, as it happened, he was in the process of changing up his life, too. Maybe he really wanted to hear that the things she dreamed matched his.

Maybe all of this was a lot more emotional than he wanted to admit.

"Books," she said at once, grinning as if they were playing a game. "I would love nothing more than to open up a bookstore right here in Cowboy Point. Nothing's worse than wanting new books and being snowed in up here. And yes, I know we have a library, and I know the librarian personally, but I still do have to give those books back."

Ryder leaned forward, and took her hands in his.

"Baby," he said. "Why don't you do it?"

She looked startled. "What? How would I do it? I have two little boys. I clean short-term rentals."

He gestured to the bookcases on all the walls. "You could turn your living room into a bookstore. All you need is a cash register."

She looked around. "First of all, those are *my* books. They're like friends to me. I will not be selling them, thank you. But also, I can't just… open a bookstore."

"Why not?"

Rosie focused on him, and she was frowning. "Because… it's a pipe dream. That's what pipe dreams are for. You dream of them while you do other things. Practical things. Things like being a mother and doing your actual job."

"I'm pretty sure there are people who think running a bookstore is an actual job," he countered. "Not that I'm an expert on bookstore owners, but that's always been the impression I got."

She pulled her hands out of his. "Those people probably have a lot more money, and two fewer toddlers than I do."

"I have money."

He didn't mean to say that. It was true, but money was the kind of thing a man learned pretty quick not to talk about too much, because people got funny about it.

And he watched as Rosie, it turned out, was one of those people.

"I'm happy for you that you have money, Ryder," she said after a moment. "But I don't know what that has to do with anything."

"Well." And he knew he had to be careful. He tried. "Right off the bat, I'd say that since you're the mother of my children, it should interest you. You don't have to worry so much. You don't have to pay for everything."

"This is just…" She shook her head. "I know you mean well, but I can't—"

"Rosie. I understand how hard you've worked, and how much you've sacrificed to get this far. It doesn't have to be that hard, that's all. They're my kids too. If you don't want to clean rentals, you don't have to. If you want to open up a bookshop, you should. I'll give you the money to do it."

She scrambled back on the couch, then got to her feet, looking at him as if he'd hauled off and slapped her.

This suggested he hadn't been careful enough.

"This is too much," she said, in that shut down sort of voice he hadn't heard from her in a while. Since he'd turned up out of the blue, in fact. "This is too much, and it's not right. We have to draw some boundaries. Everything has been… it's been a lot. Maybe it's too much. We have to be very careful, Ryder, and we really have to make sure that we're starting out as we mean to go on, and that really means that the only possible solution here is to take a break—"

But Ryder understood now. He saw the thing that had been in front of him the whole time.

The only possible solution, and it was perfect.

He was sure she'd see that too.

"Or," he said, getting up himself and moving closer to her, so he could take her hands again, "we could do this right. We could get married."

Chapter Nine

THE THING ABOUT being a parent, Rosie found herself thinking the next day, was that it forced you to do things you wouldn't have done otherwise.

Case in point: last night what she really would have liked to have done was surrender to all that clawing stuff inside of her that wanted so desperately to get out.

But the boys had been sleeping upstairs. And she wasn't the sort of person who had screaming fits anyway, as far she knew. She'd been sorely tempted to experiment with that. Maybe it was time to turn over a new, screaming leaf… but, of course, she'd done no such thing.

I can't think about this now, she had told Ryder, after staring at him so wide-eyed she'd wondered if maybe she'd actually died and what was left was her corpse, and that would make sense of the great *howl* of emotion and sensation inside of her.

Because he wanted to marry her.

He thought they could just get married, like that wasn't… Like she hadn't given up on that as a possibility a thousand times over the years and how could he possibly imagine that he could just swan back into town and *touch* her and—

Just as long as you think about it, he had replied, looking and sounding completely unbothered, which was maddening.

Trust Ryder Carey to suggest marriage and then seem not to care that much what her answer might be.

If he hadn't currently been in total possession of her heart, however unwillingly on her part, she might have tried to kill him.

But again, she had children. *His* children, who had only just met their father. She couldn't be the reason they lost him again.

He had left not long after, but not before he'd kissed her goodbye. And being Ryder, he had made an entire production out of it, leaving her limp and silly on the couch.

Which, naturally, only made things worse.

Rosie had stayed there for a long time, not sure if she was about to burst into tears, give into that screaming fit that she was sure was *just there* within reach, or somehow find a way to breathe normally again.

She hadn't really been making any progress on any front when Matilda came in, with a cat in a carrier and the usual spate of promises that the animal would only stay until she found it a home, or a shelter. This was a relief, because it had given Rosie something else to think about. Namely, that the arrival of any animal in any condition at all meant that Matilda would add it to her little menagerie in their outbuilding out back. The one she had spent one summer transforming from a makeshift toolshed sort of structure into a refuge for the animals she loved so much in any weather, all the while claiming that she would never use it for that purpose.

My intention is to open an actual shelter, she had told Rosie repeatedly. *Not have my own in the backyard.*

It had long since become necessary to pretend that she didn't know how many creatures were out there, as it was that or get in pointless fights with Matilda, who never really *engaged* in that sort of thing. She agreed with everything and *mea culpa*-ed all over the place and then did exactly as she pleased anyway.

Still, Rosie was usually a lot more snippy about the strays that Matilda collected, despite knowing that it got them both nowhere. But last night? What a welcome distraction to have a furry, orange-colored little demon to take her mind off her own troubles.

Why are you lying around like an opera heroine? Matilda had asked before unveiling the cat.

I have never in my life been operatic, Rosie had retorted. Darkly.

Though it was true that last night she had come awfully close to singing her first aria.

Then, this morning, when what she really would have liked to do was wallow about in bed in much the same way she'd done after that night in Austin, she'd had to get up.

She'd had to be one hundred percent a mom, because neither one of her beautiful little boys needed to know a thing about her heart.

Aside from how much she loved them, that was.

What made it even trickier was that today was a special day for the boys, because they were going over to stay at Ryder's place for the first time.

She and Ryder had been preparing them, but she reviewed it with them on the way over in her regrettably much smoother-handling vehicle, because he lived in an Airstream and she knew they would think that was fantastic. She kind of thought it was fantastic herself, to tell the truth. There was something so appealing about thinking that at any moment you could simply hitch up your home to a truck and drive off somewhere.

What she'd told him last night was true. She liked it here. She intended to stay here and raise her children here. That didn't mean she didn't also understand the lure of the open road.

Rosie's battered heart got a workout on the drive over, because it had snowed again in the night. Everything looked pristine and perfect, because the hesitant March sun made everything sparkle. She remembered this exact view from the times in her childhood she'd climbed around in the lodge and had gazed out into these far-off hills. She knew these ripples of snowcapped mountaintops like waves all the way to the horizon, as far as the eye could see and then some.

It was all home, and it hurt and it was beautiful and she supposed that was an easy way to describe how it felt to love. Too hard for her own good.

Though it wasn't the prettiness of the view that was getting to her, not really. It was beautiful, but today was also a major moment in this thing that she and Ryder were doing. Or had been doing before he'd thrown a wrench in it last night.

But no, this parenting thing would continue no matter what. Rosie was certain of that. And this was the first time she was taking the boys to him, so that they could stay at his place.

The first of many times if she didn't marry him, she told herself as she drove, singing songs with the boys as she went.

She really wasn't sure how she felt about it. Not that she was concerned about them staying with him, because she knew he would keep them safe. It wasn't that. But it was one thing to think in reasonable, practical terms about the fact that they would have two homes and quite another thing to think that she was potentially heading toward a future where she only had her babies part of the time.

Rosie already knew that the years went by fast. There were only fifteen years left before they could leave the house entirely if they wanted, and she was supposed to find a way to be okay with that when the truth was, she wasn't *okay* with letting them go to their father's. That didn't mean she wasn't going to do it. She knew it had to be done. She knew

Ryder deserved time with his kids just as much as she did, and she certainly knew the boys were head over heels for their shiny new daddy.

That didn't make her *okay* with any of it.

It all seemed too precarious, suddenly. Like they were being snatched away from her and she was once again being left alone—

But there, on that drive down the far hill past the lodge and on into the hills, she caught herself.

Because first of all, that wasn't what was happening. Second, and possibly more importantly, he had offered her something to fix this problem, hadn't he?

She didn't let herself think about it as she turned into High Mountain Ranch and followed the tracks that had already been laid in the new fallen snow deeper into Carey land. She had never been here before. Or if she had, she didn't remember it. She followed the directions Ryder had given her, bumping up along the main road and counting off the smaller roads that snaked off of it until she found his. And then took the correct fork, or so she hoped.

For a while there was nothing but the thick forest all around, and the twins shrieking with excitement.

Then, soon enough, they were coming out of the trees to find themselves in a clearing so beautiful that Rosie actually caught her breath.

There was a blue sky today and the sun felt like a miracle after the last little while of snow and gloom. Everything sparkled. The snow on the ground, the snow in the trees, the snow blanketing the mountains in the distance. And Ryder's gleaming Airstream sat in the middle of all of it, a snow-dusted silver bullet looking out over the roads she'd just driven, back toward the lodge and farther on to Copper Mountain rising in the distance.

And all around them, on all sides, the mountains kept their secrets from mortals and told their stories only to the sky and the wind.

Rosie could have stayed there, staring, forever. She had the strangest feeling as she looked out at this view, almost as if—

But she couldn't indulge her feelings. Not today.

She drove the last little way, pulling up close to the Airstream. And by the time she got out of the car and went to get the boys out of their car seats, Ryder was there.

Rosie got Eli and he got Levi, and for a moment, she felt disoriented. It was like she'd fast-forwarded into that life he'd been suggesting last night. The two of them stood there for a moment, here on his land with their children and no reason at all that this shouldn't be their life every day—

Her heart *hurt*.

And the boys started squirming, so they both put them down. They immediately started running around like maniacs that had never seen snow before, still shrieking out their joy into the trees.

Rosie forced herself to look Ryder directly in the eye.

Then she made herself smile, the way she'd practiced for four years in Austin.

"You don't have to fake a smile, baby," Ryder drawled, with a look she didn't try to define in that dark gaze of his.

Meaning it wasn't a fluke that he'd said it last night. Meaning she was going to have to come to terms with what her body did when he said it. How she melted, everywhere, and wanted nothing more than to stop whatever it was she thought she was doing so she could crawl into his arms.

But she didn't.

Though she did stop smiling. "Call me if you need anything," she said, and only had to clear her throat once. "They can be overwhelming."

"I can be overwhelmed," he replied. "I'll figure it out."

There was a pause, then. She thought he was very close to saying something about last night, and what he'd said, and possibly her reaction to that. Unless, of course, he'd reconsidered, which wasn't something she really wanted to think about either. But he didn't.

Though he might as well have, because she was thinking about it, wasn't she?

It was kind of a relief to kiss her wild little monkeys, then try not to stumble as she left them with Ryder. It was a relief to get in her car, and get out of there. She drove off of Carey land, then pulled her car to the side of the road and sobbed.

Rosie sobbed for a good long while, and she couldn't have said why. Or maybe it was simply that there were too many things, all at once. Leaving her babies. Leaving them with Ryder, of all people. Ryder, who she had, at different points, vowed to hate forever.

It was all those things. It was last night. It was the fact that she was used to him now. She was used to his body and having access to it. She was *comfortable* with him in ways she never would have believed could be possible. It was already more than she'd ever dreamed could happen after that night in Austin.

Yet accepting all of that only made her sob more.

Rosie kept going until she couldn't. Then she sat up and laughed at herself. She pushed her way out of the car, letting the cold air outside crash into her. One deep breath was like daggers thrust deep into her lungs. Another one, deeper, felt sharper—but better.

She bent down, right there by the side of the road, and got two fistfuls of snow. Then she rubbed it all over her swollen, too-hot, sob-wrecked face.

It felt *great*.

Or maybe it was a shock to her system, because her next idea was on the loony side.

She stood there, cold everywhere, thinking it through.

"Are you really going to do this?" she asked herself. Out loud, out there on the top of a bunch of mountains, without a soul in sight. "It's the nuclear option and you know it."

Her face was stinging from the cold rubdown. She needed to get back in the car before she got *too* cold, and that was a fine line out this far from civilization. But Rosie desperately wanted some kind of sign—

Then she laughed again, because she was her own damn sign. She could decide on any kind of option that felt right, nuclear or not. She was a fully grown woman who didn't have her children to take care of today, and if she wanted to drive all the way out to a place that was so far from the middle of nowhere that it was more like the middle of never where, she would.

Sometimes, Rosie assured herself, a girl had to go and see her mother.

Even if that mother was Charlotte.

She climbed back in her car, and jacked up the heat to high, shivering as the blast of it hit her frozen skin. It seemed smart to wait until she was sure she would stop shivering, so she did that. Then, when she turned the heat back down to a normal level because she was starting to feel hot, she unzipped her parka, blew out a breath, and asked herself if this was really what she was doing.

"It is," she said into the quiet of her car's interior, because if she'd learned one thing from her mother, it was that some intentions required words spoken aloud to take root.

This felt like one of them.

Intention rooted, Rosie drove back toward the lodge. But before she climbed up the hill that led to it, she took one of the smaller roads that branched out and headed west. Away from Paradise Valley and much deeper into the Gallatin range.

If she was still looking for signs, she decided that one of them was the fact that someone had already driven this way this morning, which was a nice gift from the universe. It was nice to have the tracks in front of her to lead the way.

And she bumped along, cozy in the car with her thoughts, for the next hour or so.

The views were beyond breathtaking. It was normally an hour out from the lodge, though today she wouldn't be surprised if it was twice that. Because it was winter, and no one could ever really be sure what a mountain might do when it got all icy and cold.

She passed the two-hour mark and kept going, following the same tracks carefully because the road wasn't always where it ought to be. As always, she smiled in something almost like relief when the road narrowed even further. Moments later she rounded a mountain along a cliff that could only be called treacherous, and then, finally, crossed a familiar one-lane bridge over a frozen creek.

Just like that, she was there.

The trees stretched high above her, covered in snow, but there were lights in them. Fairy lights to lead the way until she saw the big archway to one side, woven together from twigs and branches and what her mother had once called *sacred energy from the mountain itself.*

Hey, whatever worked.

She drove through and entered Nepenthe Creek, the

community where her mother had lived for most of the last decade. Before that, she had been a frequent visitor—especially when she didn't want to be around her husband or his family.

Rosie had been here a lot. More than she'd wanted to, some years. But Charlotte had never been one to ask for input on her decisions.

Rosie parked her car in front of the first building, because cars were frowned upon here, tools of *the world* that they were and all. She got out and stretched, then zipped her coat up. There was more of a breeze up here and the cold was piercing, but she decided it felt like clarity.

And she certainly needed some of that.

She rubbed her hands together, did a few squats to loosen up her legs, and then followed the shoveled pathway that led deeper into the community. It was surprising that no one was around, but she didn't dwell on that. These were the sort of people who could be derailed for hours by an impromptu drum circle or the plight of a wild animal.

Sometimes she envied them, Rosie thought. Sometimes she wished she was brave enough to live outside the bonds of society, to make her own way, and to welcome whatever came with no expectation or judgment.

But that wasn't her. It never had been her, to her mother's dismay.

Rosie made her way to the cluster of buildings over near where the creek ran sweet and clean in summer to see if her mother was in the cabin where she lived these days. She went and knocked on the door, even though her mother had told her a thousand times that no one knocked in a place where they all belonged. *She* did not belong here, Rosie had always thought, but had refrained from saying. She always worried that Charlotte would take something like that as a challenge.

When there was no answer, she continued on down the path to the place the people who lived here called their temple. It wasn't a church. It was as sacred or profane as they decided it was in any given moment. It was the round building in the center of the community where they gathered each morning and night. They ate there, lounged around there, held their many groups and encounters and festivals. Jack had once called it the community Starbucks, which had not gone over well with the anti-capitalists.

Rosie walked into the temple building, all wooden and built by the hands of community members past. She could admit it was a pretty place, with its soft lights and warmth, and tapestries hung to billow and wave. There was the smell of something like curry mixed in with woodsmoke, and despite herself, it all felt welcoming.

Maybe this whole Ryder situation was mellowing her more than she'd thought.

She'd have to tell Charlotte, who had long maintained that what Rosie really needed was to mellow out and let the universe lead her, or something like that. She'd never paid as much attention as perhaps she should have.

There was the sound of voices and musical instruments from deeper in the building. Rosie knew then that the community was gathered for their morning meeting—perhaps held later today because of the snow—and, as usual, some felt that they could best express themselves by playing musical instruments in the midst of these conversations.

She dutifully shed her outer layers and hung them on a peg by the door, then set her boots in the neat lines that were already there. Then she padded in, past the outer rooms that had only ever been described to her as *multipurpose*, though no purposes were ever explained. She found the community in the huge central room with the dome ceiling that was painted with constellations, none in their proper place.

There were many familiar faces in this room. Some that Rosie had known forever, some that she'd met last time she'd come here, and some she'd simply seen in town over the summer, selling crafts and wares at the summer market. She put on her smile and looked around until she found her mother in the crowd.

"Moonshadow," someone said. More than one someone. *"Moonshadow."*

It took Rosie longer than it should have to remember that *Moonshadow* was the name her mother was using these days.

But everyone turned, so Rosie did too, and there was Charlotte. Sitting with her eyes closed, and a look of familiar bliss on her face as she *tuned in*, as she called it.

The trouble with Charlotte, Rosie thought, was that she didn't look the way some of her friends here did. As if their bodies had been crying out for the meat and sugar they'd been denied for decades, leaving them a bit gamey, as Matilda had once put it.

Charlotte looked radiant, as ever. Her brow was notably unlined. Her hair was the same strawberry blonde as Rosie and Matilda's, though it gleamed with a touch of silver, here and there. She liked to keep it full and long and flowing all around her, and when she opened her eyes to see her daughter standing there, she beamed.

"Did I forget that you were coming?" she asked in her lovely, musical voice. "I know that disappoints you."

And Rosie burst into tears.

Because her mother was a silly woman in many critical ways. Her mother was also a selfish woman, in a whole host of other ways that made even less sense to Rosie now that she was a mother herself. Yet at the end of the day, Charlotte was her mother.

Right now, Charlotte was exactly who Rosie needed.

And the thing about Charlotte was that she wasn't good at the day to day. She wasn't good at routines, or self-sacrifice, or putting other people's needs above her own. She, in fact, would tell anyone who listened that these things were her *strengths*.

Rosie had always found that debatable, to put it mildly.

What Charlotte was great at, however, was this.

A moment of crisis. An opportunity for connection.

Rosie's relationship with her mother was a necklace of sorts, one jewel-like moment strung together with the next, with nothing in between. No real parenting, but she'd come to terms with that a long time ago. And there had always been Jack.

But there was also this.

There was the way Charlotte rose to her feet in that graceful way of hers and moved across the floor, a vision in flowing white clothes—all of them appropriate for yoga, or perhaps joining a cult.

Not that Rosie cared when her mother wrapped her in a hug that smelled of weed and roses, murmured lovely things in her ear, and then led her off into one of those multipurpose rooms after all.

It turned out it was a kind of study, with beanbag-type cushions strewn about the floor on a cozy warm rug. That was where they sat. Charlotte rocked Rosie like she was a baby and didn't ask her a single thing until she sat up, wiped her face again, and let out a long, hard sort of breath.

"There you go," Charlotte said, with a nod, as if she understood what was happening on a deep, cosmic level that transcended actual communication. For all Rosie knew, she did. "Emotion is a gift, Rosie. If you allow it to do what it will, there's no need for it to storm like this, taking you out with it."

"I don't know," Rosie said. "This feels like a storm."

And then she poured it all out. She told her mother about Ryder and what had happened in Austin. Because this was Charlotte, who had very few boundaries in general and none when it came to intimate relationships, she really did tell her everything. She told her about how it had been since he'd come here and found out the secrets that she been keeping. She told her about how their relationship had shifted and what he'd offered, money and marriage, and how she'd reacted. To the money thing, and then, in a much bigger way, to the marriage thing.

She told Charlotte how much she hated all this.

Or wished she hated it, more like.

"Now he's offering the thing I've secretly wanted the most," she said, and something in her shattered, hard, because that was true. And she'd had no idea it was true until she said it out loud, raw and inarguable. "I want it, but I can't do it this way, can I?"

She wiped at her face. Charlotte only made a sound to show she was listening, though she didn't speak.

"Shouldn't I hold out for love?" Rosie could barely get that out. She shook her head. "But he's so hard to resist and he's my babies' father. And Mom..." Charlotte looked surprised, likely because Rosie hadn't called her *Mom* in years. Rosie should probably have been surprised too. "They adore him already. And how can I break their hearts? Not now, but eventually. Eventually they'll understand that they could have been a family."

That word made her cry all over again.

"Rosie." Charlotte rubbed her hand over Rosie's hair, and then rubbed circles on her back, a throwback to Rosie's childhood that made her realize this was why she rubbed Levi and Eli the same way. "Tell me about this man in ways that don't have to do with motherhood. Or fatherhood. Where does he stand in his divine masculinity?"

Rosie sighed at that. "I love him," she told her mother, because if she started talking about his *divine masculinity* she was going to get entirely too graphic. Charlotte might not care, but she would. "I've always loved him. I fell in love with him hard and fast in one night, and then I spent these years hating him because he'd changed my life forever."

Charlotte nodded, as if this was only to be expected, which was oddly comforting.

Rosie kept going. "And then he walked back into my life and changed it again, and I tried so hard to keep hating him, but I never did. I never really did, did I? I've loved him all along." She sucked in a breath, and it felt the way it had when she'd been out there in the snow. Daggers down deep. "He wants to marry me. This is my dream come true." She heard the sound she made as she sucked in a breath then, because it hurt. "But he doesn't love me."

Charlotte only gazed back at Rosie, holding the space. Another thing that Charlotte was good at.

"He doesn't love me," Rosie said again, and it didn't hurt less, but it made her feel less raw and torn apart to say it. To stop hiding from it. "And you can't love someone into loving you. You just can't."

She waited for her mother to say something that would be maddening and yet true. About rivers that always made it to the place they were heading, no matter how many rocks or rapids they found. Something about the sun that always rose, and wouldn't it be a shame if there wasn't a whole night first to make it possible to love a sunrise so much.

Charlotte nodded, as if she was thinking, and her hair flowed over her soft white garments. She kept rubbing circles on Rosie's back. But there was a look in her eyes Rosie wasn't sure she'd seen before.

"You don't love a person into loving you, Rosie. You just love them."

The way she said that made something deep inside of Rosie ache in a whole new way. Because it almost felt as if her mother was talking about all kinds of love. Even this kind of love—their kind of love.

She could swear that somewhere in Charlotte's always-opaque blue gaze, there was something encouraging Rosie to think about the fact that Charlotte really did love her. And how Rosie experienced that love was Rosie's problem.

And that maybe that wasn't as messed up as she'd always thought it was.

She could almost see it, like a glimmer of light in the middle of a long, dark night.

Almost.

"You just love them," Charlotte said again. "That's truly all you have in this world." She leaned closer. "And it's actually beautiful, my darling girl. Someone loving you back is a marvel, a miracle, a gorgeous communion of souls. But that's not what love is. Love is its own reward, or it isn't love."

Something inside of Rosie seemed to settle at that. She took another breath, then let it out, deep and long.

And it was as if that *something* in her finally let go.

As if all those padlocks around her heart had not only opened, but fallen away, and she was breathing them out. Because she didn't need them anymore.

There was no need to hide. There was only love.

She sat with Charlotte for a while, and when her mother moved to the kitchen and made them both some of that spicy, fragrant tea she loved, Rosie took it. Then she kissed her mother on both of her cheeks. She *namaste*-ed her way out of the temple, then settled in for the drive back, feeling much lighter than she had on the way out.

It was late afternoon but still light out as she came out of the back roads and onto the slightly wider and better maintained road that led to High Mountain Ranch. She wasn't supposed to pick the boys up until tomorrow, but she turned toward Ryder's place anyway. She bumped her way up along the road, feeling focused. Determined.

Ready, maybe.

Or not afraid any longer, which felt a lot like magic.

She sent her puzzle of a mother her thanks and trusted the universe Charlotte arranged her life around would deliver it. It would have to, as Charlotte didn't believe in cell phones.

When she got to the Airstream, she could hear laughter inside. She didn't knock. She walked right in and found her boys and the man that she loved desperately whether he loved her or not at his table, playing with heaps of Play-Doh.

And it was everywhere. All over the boys, in their hair, and more fascinatingly, all over Ryder, too.

He looked up at her and grinned, all slow delight, and she understood then that this had always been a lost cause. She been lost long ago.

There was only one way to find herself again.

It seemed counterintuitive. She knew that. It was impractical, and she knew that too.

But she was going to do it anyway.

"There you are," Ryder said, as if she'd been meant to be here all along. Here, with her family, covered in the muck they'd made because when they did it together, it was art.

Maybe that was a lesson too.

The boys raced over to her and put their hands—covered in that maybe not so artsy muck—all over her, but her eyes were on Ryder.

The boys were telling her every single thing that had happened since she'd been gone, in unintelligible words and high-pitched noises, or maybe she couldn't understand them because she was looking at him.

"Let's do it," she said.

For a moment he didn't get it, then he did. His whole face changed. Suddenly, everything in him went still.

Intent.

She almost wanted to shiver.

And then, slowly, Ryder smiled.

"You sure?" he asked.

"I've never been more sure of anything," she told him, and she meant it.

"Good," he said. "Because neither have I."

And they didn't mean that the same way. She knew that. But she remembered what Charlotte had told her. And she basked in the warmth and light of his kitchen, her boys jumping and squealing all around her, and that light in his gaze; the promise of everything she'd ever wanted.

Almost everything, anyway.

But maybe that was enough.

She told herself it would have to be enough.

Chapter Ten

THEY SPENT A few days debating how they should do it. Whether they should do it up, do it quick, or try for something in between.

"I don't know about a big thing," Rosie told him one night while they were sitting on the couch in his Airstream, the boys tucked into bed in back. He had her feet in his lap, massaging them. Ryder took maybe too much pleasure in it every time he hit a tight spot and she tipped her head back, groaning with the kind of pleasure he normally only heard when he was inside her. She sighed as he switched what he was doing from one foot to the other. "After all, this is kind of a cart before the horse situation."

"If you want a big party," he said, fixing his gaze on her intently, because he didn't like to think that she wanted something but thought she didn't deserve it, "with the dress and the wedding party and the blowout reception with everyone you've ever met, then that's what we'll do."

He wasn't used to this kind of thing. He had always avoided intimacy of any kind, so already, Rosie was breaking new ground with him. They parented together. They couldn't keep their hands off each other any time—every time—they were alone.

As far as he could tell, they were practically married already.

But Rosie had already been through a little too much on her own. He couldn't change that. What he could do was make sure that if she wanted the whole big thing for their wedding, she would get it. He would give it to her.

And he did not choose to examine the fervency he felt when it came to that.

"Let's just be married," she said, and he liked the way she smiled at him then. It wasn't that pageant smile she could trot out at a moment's notice, the one that made him think of plastic. This one was real. It felt like *his*.

Ryder was still surprised at how fervently he wanted her to be his, too.

"We can just be married," he told her.

And there in the cozy main room of his trailer, that seemed to hum between them like heat. Like the low note of a song only the two of them knew.

That was how, the following Thursday, they dropped the boys off with their delighted grandparents. They left them with Belinda already dancing around the kitchen and teaching them her favorite songs—songs that Ryder found himself humming immediately, because she'd taught them to him, too—while Zeke was so delighted that he seemed a lot like a man in blazing good health.

Shockingly so, in fact.

Then Ryder and Rosie drove up to Livingston, an hour up the interstate, and met Wilder and Cat there.

They'd discussed that, too. What it came down to was that while Rosie loved her family, she didn't need them at the ceremony. But Ryder couldn't see himself doing life-altering things without Wilder.

Is this a twin thing? Rosie had asked, smiling up at him. They'd taken the boys on a long walk, clomping around in the snow on Ryder's property. That meant they were now carrying two exhausted toddlers back to the trailer, all red-cheeked and sulky, bordering on full meltdowns—so they were keeping up a brisk pace.

Ryder didn't find them any less cute when they were being little monsters. He thought that had to be the genetic bond doing its thing, because he'd certainly never found *other people's* children all that adorable before.

That or he was well and truly cooked when it came to Rosie and these two small creatures they'd made. But that wasn't news.

He'd looked at them, lower lips trembling and tantrums approaching like a storm over the mountains. Then he looked at Rosie. His sparkling-eyed, happy-looking Rosie, out here in the snow. And he couldn't have said what it was that clutched at his chest, then.

When you're twin, he told her with exaggerated serious-ness, *everything is a twin thing.*

Ryder liked the way she laughed. He liked the way the

breeze played with the ends of the hair she'd tucked away beneath her warm, bright hat. He liked the way the cold brought out the color in her cheeks and how she managed to be a beautiful, delicate-looking thing while also being practical and hardy.

Before Rosie, Ryder had always been under the impression that women were one or the other. Something he'd mentioned to her exactly once, and had received a nice long lecture on the topic of women, society, and expectations.

At least, he had thought then, he could pride himself on the notion that he was not a man who had to learn a lesson twice.

Or so he hoped.

In Livingston, the notorious wind was kicking hard. Rosie had worn a pretty dress beneath her coat and now, as they walked hand in hand into the registrar, she wrinkled up her nose at him. "I haven't worn a dress in a very long time," she told him. "And now I remember why. I can *feel* that wind."

He laughed. "You should think about changing that," he told her. "Because you look fantastic. Wind or no wind."

They got themselves a license, then looked at each other as if to test whether one of them was getting cold feet. But no cold feet presented themselves, so they went right ahead and got married.

With Wilder and Cat as witnesses, they said their vows, grinned at each other, and then it was done.

Outside, the old cattleman's city of hardscrabble neon

seemed like magic.

Ryder had booked them into a restaurant, so the four of them settled in and proceeded to eat one of the best meals he'd ever had. Maybe it wasn't the food, all locally sourced and perfectly prepared. Maybe, Ryder thought, it was just that this was a perfect night.

And Rosie was his wife.

Every time he thought that, it was like the world stopped for a moment. Like it took a pause along with him, to really honor that truth.

To remind him that it was real.

"Ryder Carey, a married man," Wilder said later. They'd finished with dinner and were walking down the street, following the neon signs to see if they could get a little dancing in. After a few drinks with dinner, everyone had agreed it was a necessary component of any wedding night. "Who would've believed it?"

"Kind of feels like the pot calling the kettle black," Ryder replied.

Up ahead of them, their wives—their *wives*—were walking arm in arm, heads together, and the only thing that floated back on that wind was their laughter.

Ryder still wasn't fully on board with the addition of the Lisle family into the picture, but he had to admit that Cat suited his brother perfectly. He felt certain that the same was true with Rosie and him. He would make sure that it was.

After all, that was why they'd exchanged vows.

"I guess I never thought I'd see the day when you actually admit that you feel something," Wilder continued, still in that musing sort of voice.

Ryder frowned at him. "I feel all kinds of things. What are you talking about?"

"Do you?" Wilder's voice was bland, and his look was the same. "Because I was under the impression that your response to anything emotional was to run away, find a rodeo, and try to kill yourself on the back of a bull. Between you and me, brother, you know that's not exactly healthy, right?"

"Funny," Ryder said, letting his drawl get a little dangerous. "I don't recall you as any kind of healthy model of emotional regulation. I'm pretty sure they have names for serial one-night standers."

Wilder only laughed. "And look at us now," he said.

They made it to the bar in question. Cat and Rosie fell into a conversation with the grumpy old man sitting just inside the door with an incongruous fedora on his head—but hey, this was Livingston. Ryder found his brother looking at him with a strange expression, as the neon lit them up bright and pink.

"If she's the one," Wilder said quietly, "I hope she knows it."

Ryder shook his head at him. "You were literally just at the wedding."

"You and I are genetically the same person." Wilder's

gaze was intent in a way that Ryder didn't like. At all. "And I still find you impossible to read. Imagine how she feels?"

But he didn't wait for Ryder to answer that. He didn't seem to want an answer, and that was almost more irritating than demanding one. Ryder had to be comfortable with Wilder simply walking into the bar with the ladies, leaving Ryder to fume or follow.

He chose the latter.

And he forgot about that weird moment as the night turned into something bright and even more magical, as the four of them laughed and danced, told stories, drank a little too much, and ate enough dessert to make up for any missed wedding cake opportunities.

Much later, they all made their way across the road. They kept taking too many pictures of themselves, so that Rosie and Cat started laughing hysterically about how cold their fingers were—not that impending frostbite kept either one of them from continuing with the wedding selfies.

Ryder understood. It was pretty. They were pretty. There was snow in the street already and more coming down all around the neon signs, and when they made it into the lobby of the grand old Murray Hotel, it was like stepping back through time.

They said their goodbyes to Wilder and Cat. There were a lot of hugs, even from Wilder. And then, finally, it was time for their wedding night.

Ryder swung Rosie up into his arms and carried her up

two flights of stairs. She tipped her face into his neck and laughed until he found their room, accessible only by an old-fashioned key. Once she handled the lock, he took great pleasure in sweeping her across the threshold.

And inside, the night shifted once again. Something about being in a historic hotel made the momentousness of what they'd done here seemed press in all around them.

Ryder had married her. The woman who had haunted him from the start. The mother of his children. The only woman he'd ever come to know well, and thoroughly, and not only in bed.

That sure felt like a sacrament, no matter where they'd happened to tie the knot legally.

And so, here in this room that must have seen more relationships than anyone could count, Ryder set about making love to his wife for the very first time.

He was the one who undressed her, piece by piece, carefully and reverently. When he was done he kissed her everywhere, until she was clinging to him, her skin warm and soft. He picked her up again and lay her out in the center of the big bed.

Then he set about shrugging out of his own clothes, glad that he'd dressed up a bit for the occasion and even more glad that her eyes got that hot, glazed look as he shrugged off every last bit of it.

And when he was finally as naked as she was, he crawled up onto the bed and stretched out beside her. They both stayed there a moment, smiling so wide that he thought he couldn't be the only one whose jaw began to ache.

This time, it was an ache he liked.

He would never know, looking back, who moved first.

At first it was all reverence, all worship.

Sacramental devotion, sweet and perfect.

But this thing between Rosie and Ryder had always been a firestorm, and soon enough, they began to blaze.

They couldn't help it.

Ryder was pretty sure that it was always going to be like this for them.

The first time, they let it run hot and wild, and finished in a rush that had them both shouting so loud it made them laugh, thinking security was going to come crashing in the door.

"This can't be the first time..." Rosie managed to say, her face buried in his shoulder.

"Pretty sure you have to be selectively deaf to work in a place like this," Ryder agreed.

Rosie kept laughing until she had to wipe at her eyes. Only then did they explore the little suite they had for the night. They ate the snacks they found, sitting together on the bed, as if they'd been starving for weeks. Then they took a shower together, making each other laugh because the stall was so narrow.

Then sigh, because narrow had its uses.

The fire built again.

And the next time they found themselves stretched out in the bed instead of cramped into the shower, they took their time. The fire was there but they kept it at a simmer, and everything seemed slow. Achingly new.

When he finally let Rosie fall over the edge, she had tears in her eyes once again.

This time, not from laughter.

The next morning, he woke up to find *his wife* crawling her way down the length of his torso, tasting everything along the way. She kept going until she found the hardest part of him, and when she looked up at him, the way she smiled nearly made him lose it there and then.

He managed to hold out a while, because it was the principle of the thing. But when he was finished, he thought it was a great idea to return the favor. And Ryder might have previously defined his life in increments of seven seconds, but not when it came to Rosie.

When it came to Rosie, he had all the seconds in the world, and then some.

By the time they finally stumbled out of their hotel room into a bright, cold morning to find some breakfast, they were both a little too giddy.

"Call it sleep deprivation," Rosie said when she nearly tripped over absolutely nothing as they sat down to eat.

Or something stronger, Ryder thought. *Something much stronger.*

They drove back down to Marietta, then took the road

up and over Copper Mountain. It was particularly stunning today. The snow on the hills and the sky with layered clouds that let the sun shine through. Ryder couldn't help but take it as a good, Montanan celebration of their marriage.

"It was so much fun to take a night away," Rosie said with a happy sigh as they wound their way down into Cowboy Point, also looking its prettiest in the late-March sun and clouds. "But it's amazing how much I missed the boys."

Ryder was driving with one hand, his other hand resting so comfortably on her thigh that it was like they'd always done this. As if they'd been together for years.

He couldn't get over how it felt that way. How it really, truly felt as if there had never been any part of his life that wasn't *this*. Maybe because none of it had been as good as this, if he was honest about it. He remembered what it had been like to drive into town nearly two months ago now, filled with reluctance and apprehension but still certain that he was doing the right thing.

He wasn't sure he could remember that version of him.

Because everything with Rosie was better than anything he might have had to leave behind. It wasn't even a competition.

He hadn't even seen it coming. One day he'd been marking time and hating himself for it, because the only way out of this place involved a loss he couldn't bear to think about. The next he'd been a father of twins, and this woman—*his wife*, he kept reminding himself—was the center of everything.

What was funny was that he'd always thought that leaving the rodeo lifestyle would be a tough, hard, bittersweet decision.

Instead, he'd made it without a second thought, so much so that he hadn't realized until right now that he really, truly wasn't going back.

He wasn't missing another moment with his boys.

And he sure as hell wasn't missing any more time with Rosie.

Something he'd thought would be layered and complicated, something he'd expected would come with a ton of regret was, it turned out, so easy it felt like breathing.

But all he said was, "I missed them too."

Then, as they made their way through town—noticeably quiet today, though Rosie didn't seem to notice—and then up toward the lodge, he had to bite his cheek to keep from grinning.

He waited. When they got to the crest of the hill, Rosie frowned. She stared at the lodge that was all lit up against the sky.

"What's going on?" she asked. "Why are all the lights on?"

"I don't know," Ryder said, though he did. "I guess you better go see."

He pulled up in front of the lodge and, once again, had a

sense of being a part of that sweep of history. Of being rooted right here, right where he'd always belonged, despite how hard he'd tried to get away.

But this time, it felt the opposite of trapped. It felt like finally, he'd figured out how to be free.

He'd asked Rosie to wear her dress again today, claiming once wasn't nearly enough. And it wasn't a fancy ball gown, so she'd complied, though she'd made a lot of faces while she'd dressed for him, back in that hotel room in Livingston.

It had tested his resolve more than he liked to admit that he hadn't interrupted the show.

And there was something so Montana about her, he thought now. She climbed out of his truck almost hesitantly, stopping and frowning again when she heard the sound of voices and music from inside. She was wearing her snow boots, a pair of leggings, and that pretty, pale pink dress she'd found that picked up all that strawberry in her hair and made her glow. With a stocking cap on her head, she couldn't have looked more like a Montana man's dream if she'd tried.

The best part was, she hadn't tried. This was just his Rosie.

His Rosie, he thought again, letting it settle in hard. Like a brand.

He took her hand, the one where he'd put two rings yesterday. A ruby for obvious reasons, to keep with the red theme and to catch that strawberry goodness that he sometimes thought he could taste on his tongue, and a wedding band to match. He liked the feel of the ring on his finger, too. Last night, they'd sat in bed eating salty things, talking about how strange it was to wear rings at all, as neither one of them were ring people.

But he intended to wear her ring until he died.

Hopefully a long time from now.

"What on earth…?" she was asking as they made it to the front door, where the noise was even louder.

But he didn't answer her. He drew her with him, pulling her inside the lodge and directly into the grand old lobby.

It wasn't entirely restored. It was rustic all around the edges, but this afternoon they'd transformed it into something magical.

There were lights strung everywhere. There was a long table piled high with food, because folks around here took their potluck dishes seriously. Some of the local musicians were playing over to one side, and everyone they knew was here.

The whole town had turned out. Ryder and Jack had planned the whole thing, but it was only by the cooperation of the Stark brothers and the Carey brothers—and, no doubt, Belinda's eagle eye and flair for the dramatic—that the old place that most thought was falling down looked, instead, like a fairy tale.

Because one thing Ryder knew about Rosie was that she liked a happy ending.

He'd made sure to give her one, because deep down, he was pretty sure that was what she wanted.

Their boys were there, dressed up nice and fancy—though Levi had already lost his tie and Eli looked like he'd tried to wrestle his coat into submission—and when they came charging over to hug on them, shrieking in all that ear-splitting joy, Rosie stopped pretending she wasn't crying.

Ryder hooked an arm around her neck, kissed her face, and said, "I decided we needed a big thing, after all."

"It's perfect," she told him in a low, choked voice. "It's everything I said I didn't want, Ryder, and I'm so glad you did it anyway."

He took pleasure in the way she looked around, taking in all the people who'd come out for her this afternoon. He saw her smile at her family, his family. It widened as she saw all the friends who never would have missed this, her mother and an assortment of folks from the community out in the boonies.

And then he watched that smiled dim as she looked at some of the other townspeople, like that Gwen Sheen. She was standing in the corner with her mother, both sets of their eyes a little bit bright with an avid sort of speculation.

It wasn't nice, whatever they were thinking over there. Ryder would have ignored them the way he'd done in the feed store.

But he saw the way the Rosie looked at them, and then looked down.

"Don't pay attention to them," he told her, putting his mouth to her temple again. "They both like to run their mouths. Like mother, like daughter, I guess."

The little twins had toddler adventures to take care of, so off they went in a rush, safe in this room with so many watchful adult eyes. Once they were off, Rosie turned to him.

Her eyes were so full. She reached out and took his hands.

"I want you to know, it's okay," she told him. Very seriously, he could see.

Like these were new vows.

"What's okay?" he asked, because somehow, he didn't think she was talking about Gwen and Marla Sheen, of all people.

Rosie moved in closer and tipped her head up, a lot like she was about to whisper love words. He would have liked that just fine, but she didn't.

"It's okay that you don't love me, Ryder," she told him instead.

And not for the first time in her presence, he felt as if he'd been cut in two.

He couldn't speak. He couldn't breathe. It was that same terrible feeling all over again, tossed high into the air and ready to hit ground, so hard, that he might just consider it lucky if it killed him on the spot.

Meanwhile, she was still smiling at him, softly. That

made it worse. She was still wearing that silly, bright hat and her puffy coat.

She was the prettiest thing he'd ever seen. He'd thrown her a wedding party because he'd wanted to see her smile. He couldn't make sense of what she was saying to him.

"Rosie—" he began.

But she reached up and put her fingers over his mouth, quieting him like he was one of their kids. Only unlike them, he actually went silent.

"It's okay," she said in that same quiet, serious way. "What matters is that you love the boys. Good marriages have been built on less." When he started to argue, there against her fingers, she shook her head. "I knew when I met you that night in Austin that you weren't a man who stayed put. I accept that. I want you to know that I'll always be here, no matter what. Because I love you, and I'm not a doormat. That's not what I'm talking about."

She looked away for a moment, and he did too, catching a glimpse of her mother across the room. When he looked back, Rosie seemed more resolved.

"I intend to love you forever, Ryder," she told him. "And that means all of you. You don't have to stay here in Cowboy Point to prove anything. Not to me."

He thought he would have liked it better if she'd actually hauled off and sucker punched him.

Ryder felt something almost volcanic inside of him. He was almost certain that he was going to erupt.

Because he couldn't stand that she believed that he would treat her like that. He couldn't stand that she believed he was so cold.

She didn't just *believe* it. She *knew* it. This wasn't even resignation. She'd *accepted* it.

He took the fingers she had at his mouth into his, and kissed them. Then he looked around and really took stock of the way the townspeople were looking at them. There were those who looked happy for them, but he was related to most of them.

Otherwise, there was a lot of that speculation.

He thought about what that Gwen had said to him. The word she'd used. *Trapped.* He thought nothing of it, but clearly, Rosie did.

Just because she hadn't told him about the things she might have heard, that didn't mean she hadn't heard them.

He thought about what Wilder had said to him, as if even his own twin doubted him when he'd just watched Ryder get married. And he thought of what else his brother had said—that suggestion that Ryder was hiding his feelings.

The thing was that he'd never thought of it that way. He wasn't hiding from anything. He simply preferred to work out the things that haunted him with a high-octane sport that required every single bit of his attention, which meant he couldn't think about anything else.

When he'd been eighteen, that had meant he didn't need to think about his home. About how much he missed it, when he'd been so fired up to get away. About the death of his mother, which he'd carried with him everywhere, and not because Belinda wasn't wonderful. Both things could be true at once. He would miss his mother forever. He loved Belinda as another mother.

But it was easier to ride bulls than it was to talk about those things.

And he'd decided that he preferred anonymity to small-town fame. Because as the song said, everybody here had that fame. They didn't need a tabloid. They had each other. They gossiped happily in the streets.

The streets were one thing. His Rosie's wedding party, on the other hand, was something else.

Ryder decided that it was high time he set the record straight.

Chapter Eleven

ROSIE FOUND HERSELF holding her breath, not sure what Ryder was going to do next.

She had never seen an expression like this on his face before. He looked... taken aback, maybe. At first. But then he'd looked around the lodge as if he'd never seen it before. Or had never seen all the people crowded into the expansive lobby before, when she knew full well he knew every single one of them.

It had seemed as if he'd looked at every single one of them and as he had, he'd changed. He'd stood a little bit taller. A kind of resolve seemed to settle over him. It was the exact opposite of what she'd expected when she'd said what she'd said to him.

She hadn't meant to say anything like that, and especially not after the sheer delight of Livingston. Rosie had been so nervous, thinking that they were just doing this to get it out of the way for the kids—or he was, anyway—and there she was with her overfull heart that might capsize her at any moment.

The whole drive to Livingston, she'd done her best to manage her expectations. She'd told herself, firmly, that she

Rosie didn't want to let him go. She didn't know what he planned to do, but she had the strangest notion that she *had* to stop him, that he would ruin *everything*—

But she caught her mother's calm gaze from across the room. Charlotte was dressed in flowing shades of pink and orange this afternoon, and that seemed to underscore the way she looked at her daughter from afar. Beside her, Matilda was talking to Tennessee Lisle as if she couldn't see his customary scowl, but Charlotte was looking straight at her.

Rosie could practically hear her mother speak in her head. *Practice non-attachment*, Charlotte would say. It had never been helpful.

Yet today, it was. Rosie decided to simply… wait and see what Ryder did instead of trying to predict it and run around it and get out in front of it. This was *actually* giving the man freedom, not just talking about it.

This was putting her money where her mouth was. No matter how hard it was.

She let go of his hand. She even smiled, and not the way she'd learned as a sorority girl. Ryder smiled back, but he still looked *resolved*.

He turned around and made his way through the crowd, nodding at folks as he passed them, but not stopping. He went over to the band, said a few words to the singer, and then took the mic.

Rosie was staring at him, deeply surprised that he felt this was the time to make a speech. Or that any time was a good time to make a speech, really.

She looked around again, surprised to find Wilder and Cat and the rest of the Carey family on one side of her. And then on her other side, Sara Jane came to stand beside her, flashing that silver gaze of hers all around in her best librarian fashion, as if expecting lip from their friends and neighbors. Before Rosie could tell Sara Jane that it was perfectly fine if she wanted to get back to one of her intense conversations with Atticus Wayne, the sheriff's deputy, and his fascinating sister Esther who fancied herself some kind of amateur detective, complete with a true crime podcast, Matilda came and pushed her way between them. She smiled apologetically at Sara Jane, then slid an arm around Rosie's shoulders and kissed her on the top of her head.

"So," she said, directly into Rosie's ear. "Anytime you want to share the details on how you got Ryder Carey to the altar…"

"Oh, that's easy," Rosie said in the same tone. She grinned at her older sister. "Just go get knocked up. Works like a charm."

They both laughed at that, despite the quelling look that Jack sent their way as Ryder began to speak.

"I sure appreciate everyone coming out tonight," he said, and he seemed to know exactly how to hold a microphone so that his voice filled the lobby without any feedback or other mishaps. Because of course he did. "I know this was all a lot of short notice, but when Rosie and I decided to get married, we didn't want to wait any longer."

He nodded towards Levi and Eli, who had crept up toward the stage. They were now sitting there before it, gazing up at him as if they expected him to start pulling rabbits out of hats, or some such thing.

Ryder grinned down at them, and wasn't that a picture. Such a gorgeous man and his two ridiculously cute little boys. Rosie's heart thumped at her so hard she was surprised everyone couldn't hear it.

"There was some concern," Ryder drawled, "that if we waited any longer, they'd be in high school."

That got a laugh from just about everyone.

To Rosie's right, she heard Zeke laugh too, as if he was surprised. "Who knew that Ryder was charming?" he asked.

"It's alarming," Harlan agreed.

Boone and Knox raised their brows at each other, but Wilder, Rosie noticed, only smiled. And maybe held onto Cat a little tighter.

"I know that I haven't necessarily treated this place as well as I should have," Ryder continued, and nodded in a way that seemed to take in not just this lodge and these people, but the whole of their lovely valley outside and down below them, and maybe the better part of Paradise Valley, too. "I knew when I was a teenager that I had to leave fast or I'd be held here, and it's not that being held here is bad thing. I hope I never gave off that impression. I just had that itch to get out and see the world a bit. I wanted to wake up where no one knew me, and spend days without ever hearing my name spoken out loud. I wanted to see what the opposite of a place like this felt like, and I did." He smiled. "I can't pretend I didn't enjoy it. I know some of you here today have never seen the ocean, and I think that's a shame. It has a pull on a person, a lot like these mountains that we all know have always had that kind of hold on us."

There was a murmur of agreement, from those who'd traveled their share and others who Rosie knew had never seen another state, much less a whole ocean. She agreed with Ryder that it was a sad thing that some folks had never gone that far away from these mountains.

She'd seen the ocean down in Texas. Her sorority sisters and she had often made the drive down to the Gulf and she could still remember the first time she'd walked down to the water's edge and put her feet in the ocean. It had felt so huge. So overpowering.

It had felt a lot like falling in love.

Rosie remembered the warm Texan sun on her face and the clear water off Padre Island. How she'd felt inside out. She'd wanted to run straight out into the ocean. She'd wanted to let it carry her away.

She felt the same way tonight, listening to Ryder—her *husband*, she reminded herself. He was *her husband*, and that felt as tremendous and important as it had to stand there as an eighteen-year-old girl from Montana who'd never seen the ocean before and soak it all in, thinking her whole life was ahead of her the same way all that water was, stretching out to meet the sky.

"This time," Ryder was saying, "I came home to stay. I'm not a young man with a wild soul like I once was. I've done my time in the bull-riding ring and managed to walk out on my own two feet, which is more than a lot of us can say. I want to settle down, spend time with my family, and build myself the sweet little life I'm pretty sure I've been running toward all along, right here where I know from experience that life is pretty sweet already."

"Hear, hear," Zeke boomed into the crowd, going out of his way to make sure his voice carried, Rosie was pretty sure.

Straight over to the Sheen family, unless she was mistaken, which only made her wonder what they'd said *not* to her face.

"But if I'm honest," Ryder was telling the crowd, "what I've been running toward all this time only became clear to me when I saw the prettiest girl in Cowboy Point—and in all the world, I reckon—in Austin."

Next to her, Matilda squeezed her harder and Rosie found that it was suddenly hard to breathe. She told herself it was all the eyes on her, but she was used to that. The only pair of eyes she really cared about were Ryder's.

He stared straight at her, as if they were all alone in this grand old room her brother—and probably her cousins, to give them their due—had made pretty again.

"I loved you then, Rosie," Ryder said, right there where everyone could hear him. And where *she* could hear him too. "I love you now. I looked at you and I never wanted to look away. Then we went ahead and made the two most perfect baby boys in the entire world."

He looked down at his sons, still there at his feet, and they both cheered too. Likely because the people around them did the same, and Rosie thought that it was the cutest thing she'd ever seen.

She wanted to cry. Or maybe she was crying.

"Things didn't move in a straight line for us," Ryder told the crowd. "It's my observation that the best things never do. And I imagine some of you spent the years while things were twisted coming to some conclusions on your own. I can't blame you." But his tone suggested that, really, he could. And did. "So let me make sure we're all on the same page. I'm the one who had to convince Rosie to marry me. And when she finally, graciously consented, we decided that it made the most sense to take this thing that was a little too public and keep it private. Something that was just ours, since even that magical night in Austin is a story people tell these days, and not always in the way I would. So let me do it now." He looked at Rosie again. "We were both there, so we know. It was unexpected. It was beautiful. It was love, and I messed it up, because that's what foolish men do. Rosie came back here and when I moved home too, I went after Rosie."

By this point, Ryder's gaze was on the Sheens in the corner, and he didn't pretend otherwise. By the same token, Rosie stopped pretending she was doing anything but sobbing, her hands over her mouth.

"As some of you may have noticed," Ryder said, with a hint of that grin when he looked back at the crowd, then back at the twins, "Rosie and I managed this level of perfection outside of marriage. Just imagine what we'll do now."

He left the mic with the band, and cut his way through the crowd again. He walked straight to Rosie, inclined his head at Matilda and Sara Jane on one side, his family on the other. Then he pulled Rosie into his arms.

Then, just for her—although he clearly didn't care if everyone else heard him—he bent closer to her and fixed her with that beautiful gaze of his.

"I love you," he said, very distinctly, just in case she'd decided to believe she'd mistaken what he'd said into that mic. "I appreciate you setting me free, but I'm not going anywhere."

"Ryder…" she whispered, and she was sure her mascara had to be all over her face, but for once she didn't care. "Ryder, I—"

He reached over and put his fingers over her mouth, and it made her breath hitch.

"I've got a few years to make up for, to start," he said. "And I like the team that you and I have built. You're already a good parent and I think I can be too, one day, and together?"

"You're a *great* parent," she told his fiercely, fully aware that it was the greatest compliment she could give anyone, but especially him—because the only parenting he was doing was of her boys. *Their* boys.

"All I want is a shot at forever, and I don't care what that looks like," Ryder said in that low, intense, gorgeous voice of his. "Rosie, baby, you have to know by now that all I really care about is that I get that forever with you."

Chapter Twelve

R OSIE WAS CRYING, but Ryder got the feeling that it was
for the right reasons.

She confirmed it, going up on her toes and pressing her
mouth to his. "It's you and me," she told him, with a rough
sort of certainty in her voice that made everything in him
sing. "All the way."

He pulled her out into the middle of the lodge floor and
when he did, the band started playing a sweet old country
song in their honor. And Ryder danced with his Montana
girl, knit hat on her head and snow boots on her feet, and
twirled her around and around until they were both dizzy.
Again.

And laughing the way he hoped they always would, like
there was nothing else on earth but the two of them.

Then everyone else joined them to dance some more, but
the twins came and climbed on their feet and decided that
was dancing. So it was the four of them, the way it should
have been all along and would be, going forward.

Until they were more than four.

And it wasn't that it was suddenly less scary, all this intimacy that he'd been avoiding all of his life. It was Rosie.

Rosie was worth stepping out into all that intensity. Rosie was worth not running.

This was them. This was the family they'd made together, with a few years in there of solitude to make them really understand how special this was now.

He had already missed too much of his sons' lives. He did not intend to miss another moment.

And he didn't.

Ryder used to ride bulls. He knew that he could do anything, seven seconds at a time. And that was exactly what he did.

He invested in his new life, his new family. The first thing he did was invest in the lodge project, because as much as Rosie had just become a Carey, he'd also become a Stark.

Something he made sure to say at a big Stark family dinner, just to see all the cousins wince. It was glorious.

But later, when he found himself with the three Stark brothers, they all gave him a chin lift. He raised his in return.

"Long as she's happy," Noah said, all tough guy.

"Spectacularly happy," Logan added. "Not just run-of-the-mill, everyday happy. This needs to be on a different level."

"So happy it hurts," Wyatt agreed.

The old Ryder might have laughed and told them to take their best shot. But this Ryder knew that these were men who took family seriously. Whatever it might look like to outsiders, they'd done their best to take care of Rosie and the boys.

That meant something to Ryder. It mattered.

"I appreciate that I have you three to keep me on the straight and narrow," he told them, seriously. "It's good to know that if I mess up, you'll be right there."

"Depend on it," Wyatt said, but he grinned.

And when they all finished slapping each other on the back, Ryder was pretty sure that he was considered an honorary Stark.

Just as long as Rosie stayed happy, that was.

He encouraged Rosie to open that bookstore. "Why not build it in one of the empty outbuildings up at the lodge?" he asked. "Make that the permanent store. And while you're at it, why not have a movable, pop-up store? Isn't that the big thing these days?"

Maybe he shouldn't have brought up the subject while they were packing up her house to move her and the boys into that Airstream with him. She looked at him over a pile of boxes and shook her head.

"You never seem like a dreamy type. And yet."

"All I'm saying is that there's going to be an Airstream available soon. It might as well be yours."

"I just don't think—"

"Baby," he said, and calling her that always made her melt. He could see the way her eyes went unfocused. "Do you remember signing a prenup?"

Those gorgeous blue eyes of hers focused, then narrowed. "You know that I didn't."

"Then it's all your money too." He shrugged. "Might as well start spending it."

When she made that face, he went over to pull her into his arms and lay kisses all over her face.

"It's okay to have dreams," he told her. "We're having them together this time. It's not going to be you on your own in this or anything else. It's *us*. I understand if you don't believe that. But you'll see. I'm not going anywhere."

She sighed against his mouth. "I do believe you. I really do."

He tipped her face back and smiled down at her. "Good," he said. "Because while we're talking about the future and building out the things that are important to us, why not build out our family, too?"

Rosie looked up at him, and at first she looked something like stunned. Then, as she continued to stare at him, a wild kind of warmth seemed to take her over. He watched it dawn in her eyes like she was making her own sunshine.

"Really?" she asked, her voice barely a whisper. "You want another baby?"

And he understood that once again, they were going back to the beginning. He wasn't going to knock her up this time and leave her to it. They were going to talk about this. They were going to have a baby or they weren't, but it was going to be something they did together. Every step of the way.

They just kept making this brand-new.

"Baby," he told her, his voice low and dead serious, "I want everything. And this time, I'm going to be there for every single moment."

Later, he would maintain that he got her pregnant then and there.

Because by the time they broke ground on his land in April, when the ground was a little less frozen, she'd already missed her period. And they were going to have to wait a while to be sure, but they were both pretty convinced that it was another set of twins.

"You're going to have to build that house pretty quick," she told him, as they sat together on that couch in his Airstream, tangled around each other while the boys slept hard in the next room. "And the way we're going, you better put in a bunch of extra rooms. We might get really crazy and decide we want to try a third time, so we should plan right now for that to turn into two as well."

But she didn't sound panicked. On the contrary, she smiled at him as if this was every dream she'd ever had, coming true.

He intended to see to it that they did. He was Ryder Carey, after all, the hometown kid who made himself a star on the circuit, so he knew a thing or two about dreams coming true. And he had four brothers who could help him build her the house she wanted, to start.

"Rosie, love of my life," he told her, nipping at her chin to make her laugh, "it would be my pleasure."

And then he made sure, that night and every day forward, that it was her pleasure, too.

Epilogue

THERE WASN'T MUCH Zeke Carey liked more than a good wedding.

Belinda had been muttering about missing the exchange of vows since she'd heard it was happening, but Zeke wasn't particular. Just give him the happy couple—especially if one of them was a son of his—and a little bit of a party, and he was good to go.

He had such a good time in the old lodge that night that Belinda had to warn him to settle down.

"You don't exactly look like you're at death's door, do you, while you're out here two stepping like a fool," she told him.

While two stepping along with him.

But he took her point. Though with three sons down, he had to admit that he was feeling his oats.

"I hope you're ready for what's next," he told her as they walked from the center of the makeshift dance floor. He made sure to look like he was holding onto her, as if he needed her to keep him upright.

Belinda shot him a look, her eyes dancing. "Don't you threaten me with a good time, and Zeke Carey. I let you lead the way with Alice's boys, as was only right and proper. But now? It's time for me to tag in."

And when she looked into the crowd of people and indicated Boone over by the food table, talking intently with Sierra, as always, Zeke laughed. And then laughed even harder when she turned in the other direction to find Knox in a loose group of folks who didn't know, yet, how much they would miss being so young and so beautiful. Though to Zeke's eye, Knox looked like he was going out of his way not to interact with that pretty new doctor.

"This last year of my life sure has been interesting so far," Zeke drawled.

Belinda turned back to fix him with that same look of hers. "I suggest you make certain to stay healthy, my love. Or you will wish this year really was your last."

He was still laughing about that when he wandered away from the party, and down one of the hallways toward the bathroom. Zeke had always loved this old lodge. He and his Alice had come here while the Stark grandparents were still around to run it. He thought of her as he walked, because he thought about her always.

But specifically here. On a night like this, when they'd gone ahead and married off all three of their sons.

He saw the bathroom down one corridor but he turned the other way, stuck his hands in his pockets, and let his memories lead him down the hall that was less cared for, maybe, than the others. But he could still see the care that had once been put into the worn wooden floors.

And there were still those pictures on the wall. He smiled and looked more closely because if he wasn't mistaken…

He found the picture he was looking for, small and easily overlooked, there on the wall with so many others.

Zeke looked at it and smiled. Then he reached out to touch her pretty face.

His Alice. His sweet, lost Alice, young and bright and wreathed in smiles.

They'd come here on their first anniversary. Zeke had saved up all year to make sure that they could splash out. They done it up. They'd stayed in a fancy suite and had eaten their meals in the overwhelmingly quiet and glamorous ballroom, too upmarket for a cowboy and his lady. Or it had seemed that way to him at the time, anyway.

Alice hadn't been able to stop laughing, certain that at any moment someone would see that she was using the wrong fork and toss her out.

Afterward, they'd walked in this very same hallway, holding hands and talking about all the gorgeous things their future would hold.

"Some of them came true, my love," he told her now. "Some of them you got to see on this side, but I know you're watching from where you are. I couldn't have done it without you."

And for a perfect moment, Zeke was sure that he could hear her laughter once again. It rang in him like bells and he felt his eyes go damp, because he was always so afraid that he would lose even that. Even such a sweet memory as the sound of her laughter.

He let it wash all over him. When it was done, he nodded his thanks, leaned forward, and pressed a kiss to the dusty old picture of the two of them.

"We did it, Alice," he told her gruffly. "We married them off and I'll tell you, they're all as happy as we were. It's your turn now. You make sure they get more time than we did. You make sure of it."

When he made it back to the ballroom, his wonderful Belinda was waiting for him. She took one look at his face and wrapped her arms around him.

"Had to have a talk with Alice about our great victory tonight," he said, a little more gruffly than he intended.

"She'll take it from here," Belinda replied, because she'd always known, his Belinda. She'd always understood. Alice didn't haunt them, Alice was a part of them. Alice was everywhere and that took nothing away from his and Belinda's life or marriage.

It had only ever enhanced it.

Like right now. "She'll take it from here," Belinda said again, nodding, as if she was already strategizing in her head. "She's on baby duty now. Making sure they'll come in healthy and happy."

"That's assuming Harlan ever decides to spill the beans," Zeke said dryly, because it would take a blind man to miss

Kendall's condition at this point. They all lived on a ranch, for God's sake. They knew a pregnant female when they saw one—

But they'd tiptoe around it until the happy couple was ready to share. That was the right way to handle it, Zeke knew, though he couldn't say he liked it.

"Maybe you haven't met your oldest son," Belinda was saying, with that smile of hers. "He makes caution look reckless."

Zeke laughed at that, so hard that heads turned. Belinda swatted his arm. "You really have to act more sickly."

"I'll try," he promised her.

But not tonight. He let his gaze move around the room, finding his sons and his beautiful new daughters-in-law. He looked over to his youngest son, and wondered if he might be the one who handled his own business before Zeke got around to it.

He doubted it.

Because the first thing on his agenda was the enduring problem of his and Belinda's first child. Dependable, long-suffering, deeply loyal to a fault Boone.

Belinda and Zeke agreed. It was high time for his dance around that pretty Sierra Tate to end.

One way or another.

The End

If you enjoyed *The Cowboy's Secret Babies*,
you'll love the other books in…

The Careys of Cowboy Point Series

Book 1: *The Cowboy's Mail-Order Bride*

Book 2: *The Cowboy's Forbidden Bride*

Book 3: *The Cowboy's Secret Babies*

Book 4: *The Cowboy's Best Friend*
Coming Soon!

Available now at your favorite online retailer!

More Books by Megan Crane

The Flint Brothers Take Montana series

Book 1: *Tempt Me, Cowboy*
Book 2: *Please Me, Cowboy*
Book 3: *Tempt Me Please, Cowboy*

The Greys of Montana Series

Book 1: *Come Home for Christmas, Cowboy*
Book 2: *In Bed with the Bachelor*
Book 3: *Project Virgin*
Book 4: *Most Dangerous Cowboy*
Book 5: *Have Yourself a Crazy Little Christmas*

Other titles

A Game of Brides
I Love the 80s
Once More with Feeling

Available now at your favorite online retailer!

About the Author

USA Today bestselling, multi-award-nominated, and critically-acclaimed author Megan Crane has written more than 145 books, and shows no sign of slowing down. She publishes romance as **Megan Crane** and **M.M. Crane** with an exciting backlist of women's fiction, rom-coms, chick lit, and young adult novels. She's also won a large and loyal fanbase as **Caitlin Crews** with Harlequin Presents, Harlequin Dare, Harlequin Historical, and contemporary cowboy books. And for paranormal fun, Megan partners with Nicole Helm to publish as **Hazel Beck** for her witchy rom-com novels.

Megan has a Masters and Ph.D. in English Literature, has taught creative writing classes in places like UCLA

Extension's prestigious Writers' Program, and is always available to give workshops (or her opinion). She lives in the Pacific Northwest with her comic book artist husband, though, at any given time, she is likely to either be huddled in a coffee shop somewhere or off traveling the world. Preferably both.

Thank you for reading

The Cowboy's Secret Babies

If you enjoyed this book, you can find more from all our great authors at TulePublishing.com, or from your favorite online retailer.

TULE